Strange Tales

Short Stories
By

Darren Joaquim Silva

ISBN: 0-9576401-5-3
ISBN-13: 978-0-9576401-5-3

This book is dedicated to the reader

because we're all just stories in the end…

Introduction

I still remember the first time I read a short story collection. I was 15-years old and whilst wandering aimlessly through the school library I stumbled upon 'Roald Dahl's - Skin & other Stories'
The first thing that struck my attention was the haunting front cover. What was the master of children's fiction doing dabbling in the dark arts? As I flicked through the pages I quickly discovered these were not tales for children. They all seemed delightfully dark and chilling. Every tale had a menacing twist and each one was more ambiguous than the last. Years would go by, and every so often I'd find myself returning to his many short stories.

Many people still aren't aware of Dahl's dark stories, so if you ever get the chance please read them... after you've read this book of course ☺

I've always been inspired to write a short story collection, and after writing two novels... the time has finally come.

I hope you enjoy

Strange Tales

CONTENTS

Stainless Steel Ride

My name is Edmond Pearce, and in a few hours I'm going to die. As I walk inside, the first thing that hits me is the smell, a mixture of body odor and dank mildew. I glimpse at myself in the wing mirror. My reflection distorts and I barely recognize the person staring back. All I can see is a shadow of discontent.

I was the last inmate to board the bus and my hands and ankles - restrained in iron shackles, rattle as I walk up the steel steps. The bus stretched only a few feet ahead. All rectangular with gunmetal gray decor, it was almost as if they wanted our last ride to be as miserable as possible.

The front windows were immaculately clean and strangely adorned with black curtains. A digital clock above read **12:00PM** midday.

There were five other inmates already sitting down, all wearing orange jumpsuits and faces that were stoic and protested innocence, but then again, everyone's innocent in prison. I lock eyes with the driver, a fat prick chomping down on a toothpick and glaring at me dirty. What is it with people? You see a guy in chains and all of a sudden you're holier than thou? Sanctimonious sack of shit is lucky I'm in these restraints. I bite my tongue and walk forwards.

Suddenly I feel a sharp blow to my spine. I grit my teeth and wince.

'Move it Pearce!'

I could recognize that hoarse voice anywhere. It was Frank Hawthorne, one of the correctional officers. He forever has a face like a bulldog chewing a wasp and he walks with his pants tucked into his boots thinking he's armed forces. He makes a special effort to treat the inmates like shit on his shoe. Most of us just refer to him as thorn, since he's always been one in everyone's ass.

His baton digs into my spine.

'Don't make me repeat myself shitbag!'

It's my last day alive and the last thing I want is confrontation. I quickly scan the bus for a place to sit. I choose a seat three from the back and edge in near the window. The glass is decorated in metal bars but at least you can stare at freedom. I just want to be alone with my thoughts, away from everyone and just have time to contemplate.

Hawthorne approaches me like the grim reaper and straps the seatbelt as tight as he can. I veil my discomfort but the strap feels like a python coiling around my limbs and suffocating my soul.

'If it were up to me you'd be sitting on the floor, just a shame they wrap the prisoners in cotton wool these days.' He finally lets go and not wanting to show weakness I gaze through the window until he walks away.

There was no sunlight and I could see myself in the reflection. A face with miles and dark circles around blue eyes. If you glared long enough you'd see the ominous stains from a life of regret and loneliness... self pity had rubbed me raw over the years.

The front doors open and another C.O. boards the bus. It's Vincent Winter. He makes sure the door is closed behind him and I can't help but smile softly. Winter was one of the nicer C.O.'s in the penitentiary. His blue uniform was always a few sizes bigger than his frame, but he was a family man like me, so he had my respect. He catches me staring at him and gives me his blessing with the slightest of nods.

I look out the window and anticipate what the outdoors will look like. It'd be nice to see some green meadows and blue skies... freedom really is overrated until they take it. Suddenly someone grabs my shoulder, I instantly tense my muscles and clench my fists - an instinctive habit picked up in the joint. But glancing over my shoulder I realize it's Winter. Normally his cheeks are red, with barely perceptible eyebrows and small locks of ginger hair that would seep through his cap. Today his face seems paler than usual, almost making the hue of the bus lighter.

'Thought I'd check up on you before we set off.'

'I'm okay boss, I just wanna get it over and done

with.'

'You got any relatives coming down to say goodbye?'

'My folks will definitely be there.'

'What about your boy?'

I bite my tongue and turn to the window.

'How long is the ride?'

'You really wanna know?'

'Yes.'

'Should be around one hour depending on traffic.'

'I hate long journeys, I always get pins and needles.'

'Don't worry, it'll all be over soon.'

I flash him a surprised look and contort my eyebrows.

'No, I didn't mean it like that, I meant...'

'I know what you meant boss, I'm just messing.'

I allow a wry smile to take over my face and we both laugh in the dry humor until he finds his seat.

There was a loud bang on the side of the bus and I see a guard give Hawthorne the all clear. The driver turns on the engine. I was sitting above one of the wheels and I could feel the vibrations rattle the underside of my seat. An annoying beeping sound emanates from somewhere and I look around to find it. No luck. Hopefully staring out the window will distract me.

The bus pulls out from the prison and the darkness replaces itself with light. The windows were surprisingly clear. My head rests on the cold bars whilst I attempt to disentangle the past and figure out how I even ended up in this mess.

*

'Five years I've served here, five fucking years for a crime I didn't commit! Just because all the evidence points in someone's direction doesn't mean they committed the crime. I don't care what they say about me. I didn't murder my ex-girlfriend or her stupid fiancé.'

We drove at a steady pace and it didn't take long to reach the inner city. Blue skies above us but ominous gray clouds loom in the distance. It had rained the night before and the sun was doing its best to dry the residue on the cracked pavements. My eyes scan the hoards of pedestrians that blend into the sidewalks. They're all out at this time of day - the suits, the tourists, the tramps, the addicts, the hookers, the homosexuals, it's an urban myth that they only come out at night. Staring at hoi polloi starts to annoy me, so I shift my gaze back inside the bus.

The beeping noise still pesters me like a mosquito at midnight. Where the hell is it coming from? I peer down. The seats are sticky and coated in cheap vinyl. They're torn and you can spot the yellow sponge bleeding out of them. Likely the work of previous inmates picking them in angst. But what struck me most were the five other inmates. None had opted to sit near a window and they were all deathly quiet. Maybe everyone's said all they had?

I remind myself I'm swimming with sharks, ordinary inmates you'd find in the courtyard, these guys are death row. They don't even cry when babies die, so a little injection is child's play for them.

I've brushed shoulders with some of the death row guys before. The one thing that always gets to me is their indifference. I swear to god, every full moon if you look closely at them, you'll see that fragmented stare of bleak reality, and you shake their hand and wish'em well, but you get no warmth, no emotion, just death greeting you back.

The stench of alcohol overpowers my senses and the veins in my wrists protrude again. I turn to the window and see a wino panhandling. The windows are thick as hell but the smell is so strong it forces me to spit. As we drive away, I wipe the remnants of saliva onto my orange sleeve.

I can feel people's eyes from outside the window burn into me. I glance at a street preacher holding a sign that reads: "**YOU'RE IN DENIAL**." He rambles about denying the existence of God. Somehow I don't disagree.

*

We enter the financial district and the sun is at an annoying point in the sky, forcing me to squint as it shines from behind the skyscrapers.

'Carla that fucking bitch! Always blamed me for everything. She could never accept me for who I was. I know her fiancé poisoned her mind. That piece of shit trust-fund baby hated me from the start! Trying to take my kid away from me was the last straw… he deserved to die.'

The yuppies staring at me from beyond the window only intensify my anger. They try to hide their looks of disdain, but in prison you learn the subtle art of reading faces, your life depends on it. Deep down I knew what they were thinking…

I look towards my restraints and the annoying beeping grows louder.

'Can someone turn off that fucking beeper!'

Everyone ignores me and I can no longer contain my anger. I yell out in rage and kick the seat in front of me as hard as I can. None of the other inmates flinch or take notice, so I start battering the bars on the window, hoping they'd break the cuffs on my wrists. It didn't take long for Hawthorne to come over. I'm too angry to concern myself about the consequences and I glare into his eyes. He places his baton on my face and thrusts it forwards.

'Pipe down Pearce or I'll wreck you so hard your own son won't recognize you during final visitation.'

I continue to stare at him.

'What's his name again, Darrell right?'

Suddenly all the blood drains from my face.

'That's right, I read the sign in sheet for the auditorium,' he mocks.

'Say his name again and I'll fucking kill you!'

He removes his baton from my face and chuckles as he sits back down.

We get stuck in traffic and I try to contain my anger by staring out the window. There's a pretentious restaurant with a pompous Latin name: "Qantam ad Luna" … Eating in a place like that wouldn't cost less than month's sharp wages and the portion sizes are pathetic, you're practically paying for the plate. The smell of food makes me think of my last meal order – steak and vegetables for my main, with two scoops of mint chocolate ice cream for desert.

The harsh blare of a horn interrupts my thoughts. I

peer out to a businesswoman in her Toyota Prius screaming in **anger** at the traffic. Life must be tough wearing Prada in a air-conditioned hybrid. As we drive forwards, I can't help but think how some people magnify their problems.

*

The window has a therapeutic effect on me and I realize - as I relax so does the beeping. The glass structures slowly transition to homes with boarded windows and housing projects.

The sun doesn't shine on this part of town. The streets are rife with dope dealers - raising their kids by stop signs to carry on the family business. We come to a halt at a pedestrian crossing and I stare at the Korean grocers on the corner. There were several black men and aged white women haggling for prices on the pyramids of stacked fruit.

'I have to face facts… I'm heading for death… I need to think about my options, is it still too late to cop a plea bargain? What if I can supply false information as to who really killed Carla and her fiancé? How much time do I even get with Darrell? If only I could see him now… I know his school isn't far from here.'

I start looking around the bus for any signs of wear and tear but everything just seems like Defcon 4 at the Kremlin. Hell even the seatbelt is an issue. I'm out of options and as my anxiety augments, the veins in my wrists protrude, the beeping intensifies, and I feel my legs go weak. Biting my nails is too awkward so I settle for picking the yellow sponge underside my seat.

We brake at a level crossing and I see a decrepit church with chipped paint. A limestone statue of the blessed father pierces my gaze and I close my eyes wishing the judicial system shared the same views as the Catholic Church, just say a few hail Marys and you're done. We take a sharp left turn. A tattered mattress lies against the church wall and I examine the drug deal taking place behind it.

'I just want Darrell to live a good life. My son shouldn't pay for the sins of his father.'

Outside the window, a car salesman in a cheap suit tries to **bargain** a good price for a rusty Ford.

*

I close my eyes and listen to the drizzle of rain patter the window. We come to a grinding halt and I open my eyes to discover we'd hit another red light. For the first time in my life it actually feels good to slow down, and as the lights slowly turn green, I pray they'd stay red just a little longer.

The weather now seems to match my depression and every time I blink I envision Carla. I keep my eyes closed to hold off the tears and force myself to think of better times. I vaguely remember the two of us playing on the bed when Darrell was a baby. Carla's playing dead with her brown hair fallen over her face and she'd blow it up in small whooshes whenever Darrell crawls past. That was when she used to play dead, now she's no longer playing. But even after she left me, I never washed the sheets, I didn't want to get rid of her smell around the house.

The hardest part was waking up alone every day.

I strain myself as I reminisce, but everything's just fragmented. You'd think spending five years in prison would fuel your memories but it does the exact opposite. All you have in that place is mental souvenirs, and you go over them again and again until they distort beyond all meaning. Like the same way if you keep repeating a word it soon sounds foreign.

I look to the floor of the bus and spot dozens of yellow sponge-bits scattered. I continue to pick at the seat because it calms my nerves. We're now in the suburbs - iridescent graffiti murals stain the walls while unkempt weeds burst through the concrete. They all seem to mirror my **depression**. Everyone's rushing, no one's smiling or saying hello, kids are staring down into screens – frying their brains with bullshit. Seeing all this makes me wonder what's the difference between the city and prison? Everyone lives so close… yet everyone is alone.

*

A sign in the foreground alerts me that Darrell's school is just a few miles away. He goes to a public school that teaches mostly low-income Hispanic and black kids. He's probably in class right now… if only I could see him. I'm not even sure if I can remember what he looks like. I lost my visitation privileges for numerous fights with inmates, and all I have is a torn antiquated photo of him. My folks once mentioned that his foster parents were good people and that he was scoring above average in school, so I'm grateful the apple fell far from the tree.

I keep picking at the sponge and suddenly something cuts my finger. I flinch in pain and blood dapples my orange jumpsuit. I reach under to see what sliced me and I find a tiny pocketknife buried in the sponge. I instantly sit up and glance over the seats to see if any of the guards heard me wince. Coast is clear. I hide the knife under my sleeve and control my breathing.

Suddenly the bus brakes hard. Blue and red flashes fill the window frame.

'What the fuck is going on!' yells Hawthorne.

I swiftly hide the knife and peer out the window.

Two police cruisers are outside with a cop directing traffic around a crash site. Medics are tending to people in an ambulance, and as I look further I spot an overturned car and a jackknifed gas tanker.

Hawthorne unclips his seatbelt and leaps outside to inspect the crash. I watch as he argues with the cop on duty. He puts a cigarette to his mouth in frustration then steps back onto the bus to talk to Winter. I press my face on the window and pretend not to listen.

'We're not going anywhere for around ten minutes. Apparently some jackass swerved to avoid a taxi doing sixty and he hit the tanker.'

'Wow is anyone hurt?' asks Winter.

'Who gives a shit, I hope so!'

Hawthorne lights his cigarette and steps outside to puff away. The vibrations under my seat stop as the driver switches off the engine. Somehow the annoying beeping continues.

Rain adorns the windows and red and blue flares

from the cars tint the droplets sliding down. In the flashes I analyze my story and question if I've been telling the truth. I'll admit... I was only a father to my son when it suited me, and the money I gave Carla for support was dirty. Sure some might say I provided for them, but I guess in life you're defined by how you earn that money. I sit in my acceptance and conclude I deserve to burn for my sins.

Suddenly a huge explosion rips through the street and flames engulf the gas tanker. The surrounding police cruisers catch alight and I watch as they flip over turbulently. Screams from pedestrians add to the commotion and smoke fills the air. Hawthorne, his face now covered in debris runs onto the bus.

'Shit!'

He wheezes and dusts himself then heads back outside to attend the carnage. Winter attempts to follow, but Hawthorne pushes him back on the bus.

Suddenly I realize I have to make the most of this opportunity. It's the perfect storm... I've got nothing to lose, either way I'm gonna die.

I call Winter over and show him the veins on my wrists, which were now purple and bulging.

'Jeez Edmond, are you alright?'

'I'm fine, just please loosen the strap.'

He loosens the belt and my chest expands. I make sure to exaggerate my breaths.

'Thanks boss, what the hell is going on out there?'

'Some wise guy crashed into a gas tanker.'

I shake my head and pretend to be in shock.

'You know, I haven't asked in a while, but how's your daughter? Just because it's my last day doesn't mean I have to get all selfless.'

He smiles back at me.

'She's doing great, matter of fact it's her birthday tomorrow, and I have the day off.

'I hope it goes well...'

Before he walks off, I make sure he hears me sigh.

'What's up?'

'Winter we've been friends for five years, do me a solid and unclip the belt.

'Edmond you know I can't do that.'

'Come on boss, look at me, where am I gonna go? In a couple of hours I'll be greeting Jesus. I just want my last few hours to be comfortable. Please, give a dying man his wish.'

He pauses briefly and looks at Hawthorne who's still outside.

'Fine, but you better not let Hawthorne find out.'

I smile and he whips out a set of keys and unlocks the belt.

'Thanks boss.'

'Yeah, yeah, just sit still for the rest of the journey.'

He walks away and I watch him like a hawk. Slowly I stand up.

'I'm sorry Winter, I really am.'

He turns around and I pounce on him like a wild animal. He smacks the floor and I quickly pull out the knife and slit his throat. He tries his best to overpower me but the damage is already done. He starts to bleed out, and I look away as he coughs up his own blood.

'I'm so sorry.'

I clean the stained knife on my jumpsuit and tell myself his generosity would have been his downfall someday. At least he got to be killed by a friend rather than someone who barely knew him.

None of the five inmates seem to care, nor does the driver. I take the set of keys and break free of my shackles. I also make sure to pocket Winter's gun. I crouch behind the seat and wait for Hawthorne to reemerge. The doors open and he steps in a pool of Winter's blood.

'What the hell?'

I pull the trigger immediately and a bullet bites into him. Blood splatters the windows and he hits the deck like a sack of shit. I dash over and cuff him to the metal handrail. His right ear is blown off and blood pours down the side of his face. I've killed enough people in my time so I decide to give him a pass.

'You'll never get away with this shit-bag,' he mutters.

I pistol whip him and he falls unconscious. I look out the window and notice the cops outside haven't taken notice. The beeping sound intensifies and I look at the five other inmates who stare at me blankly. I consider whether or not to free them, but I don't want any more blood on my hands.

I crouch behind the door and edge myself to the rear wheels. A low garden fence looms in the distance and it connects to the backstreets. I know this area well and Darrell's school isn't far. The only thing that concerns me is the flashy orange jumpsuit. A fire truck speeds in from around the corner and steals everyone's attention. I leap over the fence and sprint through the alley. My legs feel incredibly weak but I keep going.

Impossibly the annoying beeping follows me. It's more audible and it pierces my ears. A few people spot me but they just stare at me with complete indifference. I dash towards the school.

'I have a far cousin who lives around here. I can take Darrell and we can lay low for a while. Then maybe he can drive us to my uncle's farmhouse. Not a soul knows about that place...we'll be good there.'

I'm barely able to jump over the school gates as my legs have deteriorated and the beeping continues to intensify.

I have to be quick as the police will be here in a matter of seconds. I peer into the classroom windows. Children are working silently and I move from window to window trying to find Darrell. I spot a kid in a classroom, he catches the flicker of orange and turns to face me. A breeze blows but I don't react... Darrell... that's him.

I tap my finger on the glass and smile. His face goes from curious to mischievous and he smiles back. His angelic face void of life's troubles echoes the one I remember. He has his father's eyes and it's like looking in a mirror that reflects the past but conceals your failures. I feel my heart beating but now I can no longer feel my legs. The innocence in his face withers my defenses and I admit my guilt is as evident as the sun in the sky. Police sirens disturb the peace and I can hear them approaching from every angle. Darrell stands up and approaches the window, too young to understand what's happening. He puts his hand on the glass and I try to walk closer, but I'm paralyzed and can't move.

As I fight to walk forwards the beeping finally

decreases but its silence brings the presentiment of death. My heart starts to pound and everything around me collapses. If only my parents could see us together right now… somehow I can sense their eyes watching me.

The beeping finally stops. I feel myself slipping away, into the darkness where I belong. Life's too slippery to grasp, and I don't wanna live in a world where you need sadness to appreciate happiness and absence to honor presence. I'm done fighting, I **accept** that all of this was meant to happen – no snowflake falls in the wrong place.

I lean forwards, making sure the last thing I see is my son's smile. My eyes close, as do the curtains. Life isn't going to give me an encore.

NAME OF DECEASED: EDMOND PEARCE

DATE OF BIRTH: 14/02/1970

SEX: MALE

TIME OF DEATH: **12:05 PM**

IMMEDIATE CAUSE: <u>COURT ORDERED LETHAL INJECTION</u>

Nothing To Declare

Gordon Swan is your run of the mill businessman. He is ambivalently married with 2.5 kids, a cat and a dog. He considers himself secular and sports a simple haircut, which he gets cut every three weeks. Outside appearances may deem him to be civil, but Gordon has one fatal flaw - he simply refuses to have intercourse with the world. He is a recluse and he shuns all form of social etiquette.

However, Gordon intends on moving up the corporate ladder, and he's realizing the lifestyle of a hermit poses detrimental ramifications to his career. He spends more time at work than with his family and he despises social gatherings of any kind.

Even sitting next to someone on the bus or subway infuriates him. He is a man who likes his space.

He's just returned from a business retreat and unfortunately it didn't go as well as he'd imagined. His company had sent him on a teambuilding exercise in the woodlands. Gordon doesn't fair well with wildlife, he has a weak bladder and his digestive system doesn't agree with cold food. After urinating on a log - unaware such a lewd act would attract the foulest form of vermin to the campsite – the group was forced to flee. It rained the whole weekend and he also lost his wedding ring whilst white water rafting.

As fortune would have it, he found himself in a crowded airport. Gordon always detested flying; it wasn't the fear of an untimely death but rather sitting next to a complete stranger for an elongated time.

Not one for large luggage he scurried to security before a queue formed. He had no intention of brushing shoulders with people literally or figuratively and he handed over his passport to the security officer. The officer's movements were slow and cautionary and his face was in a permanent frown. As his eyes scanned the photo Gordon tried his best to replicate his expression in the picture.

Feeling the need to empty his bladder Gordon entered the nearest toilet. To his dismay both of the stalls were out of order. The urinals were without barriers and this annoyed him because of potential opportunists and their preying eyes. He peered around the toilet to confirm he was alone. He quickly unzipped his trousers and stuck his briefcase between his legs. As he relieved himself another man entered the toilet. Although numerous urinals were unoccupied he chose the one right beside Gordon. Whilst urinating, the man whistled and bobbed up and down. Then as he finished shaking off - remnants of his urine splashed onto Gordon's shoes. The man departed without washing his hands and Gordon squinted his eyes in contempt. As soon as he'd finished he frantically grabbed a tissue and wiped his shoes clean.

After washing his hands thoroughly, Gordon stared at himself in the mirror and straightened his clip-on tie. His briefcase was on the sink and poking out of its pocket was a book he'd been reading entitled: *"Six weeks to more friends."* It was a birthday present from his daughter – a birthday which he'd spent alone in a hotel room. The blurb detailed that multitudes of financial magnates have used it to positive effect. Gordon yanked the book from his briefcase and flicked to the chapter about smiling with your eyes. He splashed in some eye drops and practiced the technique in the mirror. He took some deep breaths and worked on his smile. After a few minutes practicing he left the bathroom much happier.

People from all walks of life poured through the arrivals hall. Gordon trudged into the sea of humanity and headed towards his terminal. Walking past the beauty stores he smiled awkwardly at the women, who appeared to be wearing the entire cosmetic counter on their faces. Screaming children bustled ahead, and a woman in a floral dress barged past him. She dropped a notepad but she disappeared before Gordon could alert her.

Finally he arrived at the departure board. The

flight information flickered and he spotted his flight.

18:00 – Seattle - 4603 – Delayed

He bit his tongue and refrained from using obscenity. Normally in these circumstances he would regress behind a newspaper, read it numerous times then engage in the crossword, but this was the perfect opportunity to meet new people. There were hundreds of humans congested around the terminal and he decided to put the books teachings into practice.

Walking around, the noisy chatter of various languages interrupted Gordon's positive demeanor, but he mustered the confidence and headed into a nearby coffee shop, intent on meeting someone.

With his espresso in hand he surveyed the shop and decided to sit beside a woman reading a newspaper.

'Doing the crossword?'

'I'm married.'

'Oh, me too, I was simply making conv…'

'Where's your ring?'

'Oh well that's a funny story actu…'

'Yeah tell it to someone else.'

She swiftly folded her paper and walked away. The sound of her heels grew faint and Gordon stared at the floor. Instantly a man took her seat and Gordon sat upright and faced him.

'Hello.'

'Je ne parle pas anglais.'

With that being the coup de grâce, Gordon surrendered and walked to the departure gate.

He stared around the lounge, several people were on their phones and some were sleeping - having folded their coats into makeshift pillows. He trudged towards the large windows and gazed out. Sunlight glistened the Hudson Bay and the Statue of Liberty overlooked the white clouds.

Gordon turned around and spotted a man sitting down. He was wearing a distinct grey pinstripe suit and radiated an aura of quaintness. With nothing to lose he sat next to him and noticed he was writing in a fountain pen, on a brown piece of parchment. His penmanship was immaculate.

'Writing a letter?' asked Gordon.

But his words evidently failed to move him. Gordon peered in closer and noticed he was writing in English. He definitely heard him.

'Notes for an article? Ah you're a journalist?'

The man remained unperturbed and carried on writing. Gordon sat in the awkward silence and after a few seconds decided to throw in the towel. He picked up his briefcase and walked away. Suddenly the man spoke.

'There we go, finished... Sorry for my unmind-fullness.'

Gordon turned around and noticed the man was now standing to greet him. He walked forwards and shook his hand. It was considerably colder than his, yet his handshake was perfect – not too firm – not too limp. 'I'm Vergil, nice to meet you.'

'Gordon Swan.'

He thought about his name and instantly felt insecure about his own. Vergil, what a great name he thought - on the cusp of enigmatic and dangerous.

'As stated, please excuse my nonchalant behavior, I'd be most glad if you joined me.'

Gordon took a seat next to him. He observed Vergil's suit. It hardly drooped and was clearly tailor-made to enhance his definitions. Unlike his, which was straight off the rack.

'You were saying?' asked Vergil.

'Oh never mind, I was just inquiring as to what you were writing?'

He folded the parchment in neat quarters and slipped it inside the pocket over his heart.

'No, neither a letter nor an article, I'm more of a biographical man myself. I hope someone has the tenacity to write one about me one day. Although I hear they only sell when you're dead!'

Gordon laughed and it went silent for a moment. Suddenly he remembered a tip from the book – find common ground as soon as possible.

'My flight got delayed, it's very frustrating.'

'Yes, mine too. In fact I arrived at the airport three hours early, so I've been sitting here a long while. But look on the positive side, now we're in pleasant conversation.'

Gordon felt relieved. Finally he'd met someone with whom he could converse with.

'Yes it's very true, I've been reading a book that details how a simple chance encounter can change your life forever.'

'You wouldn't happen to be reading 'Six weeks to more friends?' asked Vergil

'Yes! That's the book indeed,' said Gordon slightly shocked. 'How did you know? Have you read it?'

'Fortunately I have, it's a classic.'

'Has the book helped you?'

'Oh yes, very much so. One might even say I owe my life to that book.'

'Interesting. It was given to me as a birthday present.'

'Did you celebrate your birthday recently?'

'Yes on March the 1st.'

'How pleasantly strange, I also entered this world on March the 1st.'

Gordon leaned back in his chair and stared at Vergil flabbergasted.

'Wow what are the chances your middle name isn't Gordon is it?'

'As a matter of fact… no I'm just joking.'

Gordon grinned. 'So do you have a family? A wife and kids?'

'Yes, a boy and girl, but unfortunately I haven't seen them in fifteen years… I'll be seeing them soon.

'Wow I'm sorry to hear it.'

'It's quite all right… Do you have children?'

'Yes I have the same, a boy and a girl,' said Gordon. 'I'm seeing them now for three days before flying out again.'

'How lovely. Where do you live?'

'Seattle.'

'Wow I'm also flying to Seattle. It's my hometown in fact.'

Gordon again looked at him in shock and took out his boarding pass. Vergil also buried his hand in his pocket and searched for his.

'I always pay slightly more to secure the window seat – I love looking out the window, it always seems to make the flight go faster.'

'What's your seat number?' asked Vergil.

'24C.'

'Mine is… well you'll never guess, I'm 25C'

He flashed his pass and Gordon's heart almost stopped. He couldn't help but become slightly scared.

'Looks like we'll be sitting next to each other! Ah the universe can be a tricky mistress. Good thing we've already broken the ice,' added Vergil.

Gordon dabbed his sweat with his tie and stared at a plane flying into the clouds.

'Isn't it amazing? How one day man decides to bend pieces of metal together and design something capable of transporting people across the world. It just shows the power of the mind,' said Vergil.

'I never thought of it that way. Do you work in the aviation?'

'No I'm the CEO of a little company called Encantra Chemicals.'

Gordon tilted his head to the side and looked away in deep thought. 'Where have I heard that before… oh my, yes! That's it, the pharmaceutical business.'

'Ah… so you've heard,' said Vergil.

'Little company? You are modest, it's one of the biggest medicinal companies in the world. Although come to think of it, with all due respect, I did hear that it's fallen on hard times.'

'Yes unfortunately it has…'

Suddenly an announcement rung through the departure lounge.

'*Flight 4603 to Seattle is now boarding*.'

'Well look at that, the power of positivity!' exclaimed Vergil.

A large queue began to form and Gordon stood up.

Vergil however remained unperturbed.

'Aren't you coming?' asked Gordon.

'What's the rush? Our seats are paid for, there's no point following the crowd.'

Gordon sat down again. 'I wish I could see the world through your eyes. Your company may be in debt, but you're still a successful businessman and you've achieved so much in your career. I can only wish to be half the man you are.'

'You're too kind. If I can impart any advice – I'd say stay exactly as you are. Keep talking to as many people as you can. Always present yourself as a professional, and always be willing to take risks.'

'Risks?'

'Yes, just the other day I was at a casino. Most people were betting small. But you must bet big to win big. I lost, but what matters is that I'm willing to take chances. Right now I haven't got a care in the world!'

Gordon watched as Vergil's knee bounced up and down repeatedly.

'Wow, anything else you can tell me?'

'Come to think of it, I've barely spoken to anyone in a long time. If it weren't for you making conversation with me today I would have gone a whole three months without conversing with someone. I even gave all my possessions away. In life you must get rid of the non-essential. My wife used to say – "as long as you have clean underwear you'll be fine."'

A ray of sunlight poured through the window and lit the side of Vergil's face. Gordon stared at his unkempt beard and noticed the crows feet that spread around his eyes.

'Live every day as if it's your last Gordon.'

'I just wish you could take the stress away sometimes.'

Vergil glanced over his shoulder.

'I was hesitant to show you these, but you've proven to be an admirable gentleman. If you truly want to escape the stresses of life, I have just the thing.'

Vergil withdrew a small bottle of pills. He shielded them from plain sight and Gordon stared at the lurid color of the tablets. 'What are they?'

'I had these custom made before I sold my shares.'

'What do they do?'

'They'll permanently remove all of life's troubles. Easily consumed and with no side effects. I've been debating whether or not to take them for a while now, but today is the big day.'

Gordon was hesitant but thought it would be unwise to not follow instructions from such a prominent man. The book he was reading even stated one should emulate others who are successful.

'Are they illegal?' he asked.

'Well I haven't supplied them to mass market yet. At the moment they're only reserved for special occasions.'

Again Gordon was hesitant but he finally decided to take a leap of faith. 'Sure I'll live a little!'

'That's the spirit… I do have one small favor though?'

'Sure.'

'Do you mind if we switch seats on the plane? Normally I'd never ask but today I'm just in the mood for staring at the clouds.'

Knowing that Vergil was a financial tycoon he complied. One day he could return the favor he thought. 'Sure, I don't see why not.'

'Gordon, you truly are a king among men.'

Another announcement blared, this time with a more vigilant tone.

'Flight 4603 to Seattle. Final and immediate call.'
Gordon stood and clutched his briefcase. 'I guess we better get moving.'

Vergil stood and fastened his blazer. They were now the only two people left in the gate.

'You head onto the plane, I have to quickly purchase a bottle of water from the machine. No matter how lavish one's lifestyle is, plane prices will always be corrupt,' said Vergil.

Gordon chuckled. 'I couldn't agree more. Thanks again, it's amazing how chance encounters can literally change your life. I can't wait to see my family now.'

'I look forward to seeing mine too,' replied Vergil.

Gordon handed his ticket to the agent and scurried off down the hall. It was evident from his movements he was in a state of exhilaration. Vergil kept smiling and waited until Gordon turned the corner. He put a few pennies in the machine and grasped the cold bottle of water.

He pocketed the pills and stared out the large glass windows. Evening twilight illuminated the runaway and he spotted Gordon waving at him from the plane door. Vergil placed his hand over his heart and took a deep breath.

'Time to kiss the sky and die.'

Queen of the Night

With one hand on the wheel and the wind in her hair, Bella leaned back and admired the flat sunbaked badlands. With not another car for miles she slammed the gas. The speedometer needle danced as her teal 68 Mustang blazed through the empty desert road.

She removed both hands from the wheel and lit a cigarette. The sunlight tinted her red hair and she took a long drag in the breeze. The ringing of a cellphone disrupted her bliss and she put it on speaker. A nasal voice echoed through the air.

'Hello, it's your mother.'

Bella stubbed her cigarette and a whirl of orange

sparks gusted in the wind.

'Mom, I've only got one bar of battery.'

'Annabella…'

'Please stop calling me that.'

'I don't know why you insist on taking this nonsensical journey every other year. Why can't you just settle down? You've got the look Bella – the strong cheekbones, the red hair, honey skin… you could snag a handsome man.'

'Mom I'm 26-years-old. I don't need a man to make me happy.'

'Oh Bella must you be so prickly! Anyway are you wearing your seatbelt? What about food, are you eating well?'

Bella rolled her eyes and scrunched her face.

'Don't pull that face at me!' yelled her mother. 'With an empty stomach you'll fall asleep at the wheel, crash the car and that silly cactus you keep behind the wheel will stab you in the eyes.'

Bella stared at her peyote cactus.

'Okay. I'll make sure I eat something on the way.' Her cellphone beeped. 'Mom I really have to go!'

'One last thing…'

'I know, I know, you tell me every time I take this trip. Never ever pick up a hitchhiker. I won't. I promise.'

'Good, see you soon.'

She frowned as the phone battery edged closer to death.

*

The eyes of evening opened across the sky. Bella

saw a diner up ahead and pulled up on the dirt road. She made sure the car was locked. Scattered around the entrance were a number of Harley Davidson's. A dusty neon sign that illuminated a few letters read – 'Desert Legends Diner.'

Inside, the smell of cigarettes smacked her nostrils. The crackling of bacon echoed from the kitchen and a few rednecks were seated around a booth watching the game. Bella sat in shade near the window. She got the feeling the diner housed a history of bar brawls so she avoided eye contact with the locals.

The game finished and the bartender switched on the news and turned up the volume.

"The bodies were found charred to a crisp in the middle of the desert and unfortunately the cause of death is still uncertain. We'd just like to remind all of our listeners and to any one driving through the area to not pick up any wandering strangers or hitchhikers."

Bella squinted and noticed the TV displaying pictures of dead bodies sprawled out in the desert. She shuddered and realized a waitress was standing in front of her. She had a sunny disposition and a round face. Her apron was tied above a pink shirt and a necklace with a dove pendant hung above her cleavage.

'That's the second time you've ignored me miss, how about some coffee to wake you up.'

'Sorry, television's my one weakness.'

'Well let me go over the menu. We have a special on cherry pie at the moment and our soup of the day…'

'Coffee and the special sounds great.'

The waitress wrote it all down on a sticky-note. It took her a little longer than normal and Bella presumed she'd mess up the order. She turned back to the TV but the bartender put another game on to mute the yelling rednecks.

The waitress returned with her order and she placed the pot of coffee and pie down on the table. Bella handed her a scrunched ten-dollar bill and as she counted the change she dropped some pennies to the floor. As she bent over, the yokels celebrated her with an array of catcalls and wolf whistles. She blushed and Bella helped pick up the coins.

She took a seat opposite her.

'I'm Sallyanne by the way.'

'Bella.'

She poured herself some coffee and bit into a chunk of pie. The rednecks exited and some leered at the pair. Bella gave them a dirty look and Sallyanne shook her head in disgust.

'So you got a fella?'

'Meh, I prefer to ride solo.'

'Yeah I guess you're right. Besides you shack up with a guy here, I'll bet you all the cherries in that pie he'll be a psychopath.'

Bella laughed and sipped her coffee. 'So you do anything else other than waitressing?'

'I'm actually an aspiring actress. I've even enrolled in acting classes and everything.'

Bella looked at her to discern if she was serious but she was. She joked in her head that Sallyanne would have trouble memorizing lines.

The bartender overtly cleared his throat and Sallyanne sprung up. 'Anyway I best get back to work or Bill will feed me to the dogs!'

As Bella finished her food, a skinny man with a white beard ordered a coffee from the bar. In the corner of her eye she could feel his gaze undressing her. He cleared his throat to get her attention but she continued to ignore him. The man abruptly stood and the screech of his bar stool made Bella jolt. She grabbed a fork and hid it under her knee. The man walked towards the door and yanked the sugar dispenser from her table. Bella occupied herself with the menu to avoid staring at him. He soon departed and she watched him from the window until the suns rays obscured her vision.

*

Bella finished the last of her coffee and gave Sallyanne a decent tip. 'It was nice meeting you… If you finish work soon, why don't you come have a drink with me? I've got tequila in the car.'

A loud smash interrupted them. Sallyanne grimaced and Bill screamed her name from the kitchen.

'Sorry sweetie, I'm working overtime tonight! Those acting classes won't pay for themselves. You drive safe now!'

Bella's smirked and waved goodbye as Sallyanne tiptoed towards the kitchen.

When she headed back to her car, the skinny man with the beard was leaning against it. His motorcycle was parked beside him and Bella felt his gaze pierce her again.

'Can I help you?' she asked.

He popped a cigarette in his mouth and offered her one. Bella shook her head.

'You look familiar,' he said in a hoarse voice. 'Been a local here going on ten years. And you definitely look familiar… Strange, not many people come around these parts, specially since all them deaths started happening.'

Bella took out her keys and approached the door but he blocked her.

'It's dangerous out here, you should be careful.'

'And who are you? The knight in cheap leather armor?' Bella pushed his skinny arm aside.

'So it's true, all redheads do have hot tempers.' He smirked and she spat on the floor next to his black boots. The man simply smiled and watched her drive off. 'You take care now.'

*

The sun melted an orange stain into the sky. Bella drove at a steady pace and a flurry of red and blue flashed in her rearview. It was a police cruiser. She sighed and pulled over on the dirt. A cop wearing a beige uniform tapped on the window. He had an oily sheen over his face and stood like the poster boy of the academy. Bella lowered the window.

'Evening miss, no need to be alarmed just a routine stop, making sure everything's right as rain.'

'Yeah everything's fine,' said Bella.

'Now you may or may not be aware, but every other year we regretfully have "major disturbances" in this area. Do you mind if I take a look at your license and registration?'

Bella opened the glove compartment and handed over her details. He scanned them and smiled.

'Annabella Hudson eh? Why's a lady like you driving alone?'

'I've always considered myself a lone wolf.'

He handed back her documents and put a toothpick in his mouth. 'Yep I'm with you on that. Sometimes it's best to go your own way in life.'

He peered inside and Bella quickly shut the glove compartment.

'Do you mind if I borrow that?'

Bella remained silent.

'I'm all out of water and the nearest gas station is miles south.'

'Are you sure? It's been sitting in there for days.'

Bella handed him the bottle. It was warm and she grimaced as he gulped it.

He wiped his mouth and frowned.

'What's wrong?' asked Bella.

He glared at her cactus behind the wheel.

'Interesting plant.'

'You don't like it?'

'Ah, cacti just give me the creeps that's all. I grew up in these parts you see, and my ma had em scattered all over the house. Whenever I was causing trouble, my old man used to scare me, tell me these spook stories of how if I kept misbehaving he'd feed me to this special cactus. It only blooms once every so often and legend has it - that if you witness it bloom you don't live to tell the tale… The Queen something or other.'

'The Queen Of The Night,' interrupted Bella.

'You know of it?'

'I've heard things yeah. It blooms once every other year and only at night so it's a pretty rare sight.'

'Christ on a bike I used to have night terrors of its thorny vines coiling around my legs and making me slim pickings for all the rattlesnakes and mountain cats.'

'Well I'm sure you've got bigger problems to worry about these days.'

The cop laughed and handed her water back.

'Guess you're right. Just a spook story after all… Anyway you come across any trouble, I want you to call me on my personal number.'

He handed over his card and Bella threw it inside the glove compartment. 'Thanks, goodnight.'

He tapped the roof of her car and drove off into the twilight. Bella lit a cigarette and watched the cliché tumbleweed roll through the flatlands.

*

The sky behind her was dark and a crescent moon hid behind the red clay mesas. She'd been driving in a straight line for an hour and the looming darkness forced her to slow down. The coffee had worn off and her eyes grew heavy. Every few seconds her eyes closed and her chin smacked her chest. She turned on the radio to keep her awake, but all she could find was heavy static on the stations.

She turned it off and opened the window. Unexpectedly something caught her attention. A man was stood beside a smoking car and his thumb outstretched. Bella swiftly turned off her lights and drove past. She eyed him through the rearview and couldn't help but feel sorry for him.

'Crap! If I just leave him, it'll bug me all night. What the worst that could happen? Besides the conversation will keep me from falling asleep.'

She slowly reversed and parked next to him. She switched on the interior light and opened the passenger door. The man hid behind a cigarette, took one last puff and threw it into the sand. He stepped inside and avoided eye contact.

'Looks like you need a ride?'

He dusted the orange sand off his boots and shut the door.

'Where you headed?' asked Bella hesitantly.

'Same place as everyone else... the bottom of this long road.'

She drove forwards and kept trying to get a glimpse of him. He sat in silence and glared out the window.

'My name's Bella by the way,' she said outstretching her hand. He instantly grabbed her hand - his handshake was incredibly firm.

'Nate Spector.'

He finally made eye contact and Bella got a good look at him. His face was engraved in scars and his glare made her uncomfortable. He wore a dark green shirt and a pair of dog tags clanked above his barrel chest.

The silence unnerved her so she put the radio on. The news station continued its story about the recent deaths. Nate switched it off. 'Hate the news, nothing but fear mongering.'

Bella could feel her heart beating and she was beginning to regret picking him up. Again came the awkward silence that Nate seemed to bask in.

'So did you catch the sunset earlier? There was this beautiful red sky,' she muttered.

'What did you say?!'

Bella jumped in her seat and noticed him staring at her. 'I was just saying, the sunset... there was a nice red sky.'

Nate grit his teeth and turned to the window.

'Red sky... I hate everything about that color.'

'Why's that?' asked Bella.

'Reminds me of someone I'd rather forget.'

'A past lover?' asked Bella with a wry smile.

'I don't wanna talk about it.'

'Come on, I picked you up, least you could do is spare me the awkward silence...'

Bella accidentally drove over a pothole. His dog tags clanked together.

'What's with those anyway?'

Nate ignored her and suddenly started to inspect her glove compartment.

'Hey! What are you doing?!" she yelled.

He tossed the bottle of water aside and yanked the cop's business card. Bella outstretched her hand for him to give it back.

'Give that here!'

'Goddamn pig pulled me over earlier! I told him I was having car trouble but he made some bullshit excuse about an emergency at the station. I see he gave you the special treatment... I wonder why?'

'I don't know.'

'I'm sure you serviced him real good. Women always like a man in uniform.'

Bella laughed in disgust. He lowered the window

and flung the card out.

'What did you do that for?!'

'Hmm what else is in here?'

He continued to rummage through her belongings.

'What the hell are you doing?!' yelled Bella.

Suddenly Nate pulled out a 9mm handgun.

Bella froze and a feeling of dread crept up her stomach and into her throat.

'Put that back now,' she said calmly.

He handled the gun like an expert marksman and examined it under the moonlight.

'If you don't put it down, I'll brake really hard. You're not wearing your seatbelt so get ready to fly through the windshield.

Nate pointed the gun right at her. 'Make me.'

Bella gritted her teeth. All of a sudden he erupted in laughter. 'What's so funny?' asked Bella.

'Well you're awfully calm for a woman under duress, especially when you take into consideration you're being held at gunpoint by a total stranger.'

'So, what's your point?!'

'You and I both know… there's no bullets in this gun.' He swiftly ejected the magazine and tossed the gun onto her lap. 'I'm Ex-military… Lieutenant Nate Spector at your service.'

Bella gasped in sweet relief and grabbed the water bottle, but instead of drinking it she flung it at him.

'You're an asshole.'

Nate laughed and took a swig of water.

'You said ex military. Why'd you quit?'

'I didn't quit. I was… dismissed with disgrace.'

He clenched his fist and stared to the sky.

'Normally I don't trade war-stories with common folk

but my therapist says its good for my PTSD.'

'Didn't they prescribe you medication?'

Nate reached into his pocket and pulled out a bottle of pills. 'They say war is a drug, just a shame they don't tell you about the side effects.'

He threw some into his mouth and grimaced as he washed them down with water. Bella silently stared at him and pondered his scars.

'Look something's up ahead!' he yelled.

Bella jumped. 'Where I don't see anything?'

'I used to be one of the best spotters in the US military. Don't ever fault my vision.'

Bella slowed down and peered as far as the headlight lamps would allow her. She saw an overturned cop car on fire. She lowered the window and felt the heat scorch her cheekbones.

'Holy shit, it's the cop,' she added.

'Give me your gun now!' yelled Nate.

'No.'

'We don't know what's happened. Someone could be hurt. He warned me earlier about some serial killer. Give me your gun now!'

Bella wanted to drive on but her curiosity held her. Nate snatched the gun from her.

'And the bullets… just for precaution.'

Bella bit her tongue and reached into her pocket. She tossed him a single bullet. He leered at her and stepped outside. He crept towards the wreckage and Bella watched as he faded into the night.

A few minutes passed and the crackling of the fire unnerved her. She blared the horn several times in panic. Nate soon limped back to the car, carrying the cop on his shoulders. Bella opened the door and Nate tossed him inside and onto the backseat.

His face was covered in ash and he coughed hysterically. Bella quickly gave them the last of her water. 'What the hell happened?! Is he okay?'

'He's not conscious,' panted Nate. 'We need to get him help now!'

Bella started the car but she suddenly remembered Nate hadn't given back the gun. 'Give it back now.'

'What are you talking about?'

'Don't play dumb, give me back the gun.'

'We don't have time, just drive!'

'I'm not going anywhere until I have my gun.'

The cop in the backseat started convulsing and foam erupted from his mouth. Nate looked on in horror and quickly handed Bella the gun.

'There! Now drive!'

Bella remained still and scowled at him. Instead of starting the car she reached behind and searched for the cops handgun. She yanked it from his holster and put it in her pocket. Nate stared at her in disbelief.

'You can never be too careful,' she added.

The engine roared and Bella sped off. A sign on the rocky terrain detailed a service station was just a few miles ahead. She accelerated hard and increased her speed. Nate stared out the window and everything started to blur. Bella watched as he started to blink hard. She took one hand off the wheel and scooped her cactus.

'You know, there's an old legend of a mysterious cactus that only blooms at night every other year… you ever heard of it?'

Nate wiped his sweat and shook his head.

'It's called the Selenicereus Grandiflorus. In fact it's so rare that few have lived to tell the tale.'

Bella locked the doors and dangerously sped past the service station.

'Where are we going?' asked Nate.

Bella veered off the road and drove through the hoards of cactuses.

'Wait! We just passed the service station?!'

'Relax I've done this before... just a shame the waitress couldn't join us,' said Bella calmly.

The car tore through the sand and the wheels kicked up an orange storm. The stars no longer safeguarded the moon and the sounds of rattlesnakes brought a cruel smile to Bella's face.

'We're nearly there... I can't wait for you to meet my queen.'

Lydia & Livia

The mother's name was Onata Lockette but this was her maiden name. She was formerly known as Onata Osman but since her husband traded a life of family bliss for his younger secretary, she looked upon the name with great disdain.

She was a sublime woman who viewed the world through emerald green eyes, with silky black hair that drooped under her shoulders.

One spring evening, Onata found herself at home by the marble fireplace and heavily expecting. Her bump was far larger than most pregnant mothers she'd encountered, and the child's sex was shrouded in mystery. Her water soon broke and her older sister Ophelia drove her to the hospital. Although just a year separated the sisters, Ophelia was noticeably contrasted to the younger Onata. Their mother would often jest at family gatherings that Onata had aged like fine wine, but Ophelia had aged like milk. Ophelia's face was crinkled and bony and whatever the weather - her thin fingers would always be coiled around a glass of gin.

Onata was rushed into the delivery room and after much painstaking effort, she pushed out a lovely girl, whom she decided to name Lydia. Everyone gathered and admired her. But Lydia's moment in the sun was unexpectedly cut short as her mother started to contract again. The doctors placed Lydia aside and realized that a second child was on the way.

After another excruciating round of labor, the mother gave birth to an angelic girl - almost identical to Lydia. She cradled her in her arms and decided to name her Livia. But amidst all the joy, something was not right. For little Livia wasn't crying or breathing. The doctor grabbed a towel post haste and began a procedure of tactile simulation. The nurses rushed around the room and the mother screamed in fright. Fortunately Livia's loud cries soon echoed around the room. Everyone gasped and the mother held her close to her heart whilst the nurses clapped.

*

As the years went by the twins grew up healthily. Each adorned with milky white skin, silky black hair, and rich emerald eyes. The only noticeable difference was that Lydia's eyes were a shade greener. Growing up without a father proved challenging for the twins and every so often they'd ask about his whereabouts, to which their mother would always reply "He's away on business."

On the day of their eighth birthday Livia was in her room playing with her abacus. Lydia soon entered holding a doll and sat on her bed.

'I wish you wouldn't sit on the bed. I just made it,' said Livia. 'And please knock next time you come in.'

'Sorry,' said Lydia combing her dolls hair. 'Do you think dad will come home for our birthday?'

Livia sighed. 'Father's not coming back.'

'But mom said he's on business.'

'He's not on business.'

'Once I heard mom say he's in hell.'

'He's not in hell, one time when you were asleep I heard mother say to Aunt Ophelia that he's in Cancun.'

'Where's that?'

Livia rolled her eyes and put away her abacus. She walked towards her antique globe and spun it.

'That's where it is,' she said pointing her finger.

'Don't worry about father. Today is our birthday, you should be happy.'

Lydia's face lit up. 'I am… presents!'

Livia smiled and sat next to her. 'What did you ask mother for?'

'A dollhouse. What did you ask mother for?'

'Just for some more books.'

Their mother's voice bellowed from downstairs.

'Lydia! Livia! Our guests will be arriving any minute. Make sure you've washed up and put on your dresses!'

Livia walked her sister to the door. 'Hurry and do what mother says. The quicker you do, the faster you'll be able to open your presents.'

When Lydia returned to her room she found a blue polka dot dress on her bed. She slipped it on and looked in the mirror. Her cheeks blushed with excitement and she ran out the door.

On the way downstairs she encountered a woman. Her hair was pulled back and her face was powdered with red lipstick. 'Little Livia, oh how you've grown!' she said squeezing her cheeks.

Lydia wiped her cheek. 'I'm Lydia, not Livia.'

'Oh I'm sorry, well happy birthday! Where is the other birthday girl?'

'I think she's in her room.'

Without saying another word the woman brushed past her and scurried away.

Downstairs Lydia peered at all the guests. Her small head bobbed up and down as she pondered their opulent affectations. An old man wearing a brown corduroy suit accidentally barged into her. Some of his champagne trickled into her hair.

'I beg your pardon… Oh if it isn't Livia!'

He took out a handkerchief and dabbed her dress. Lydia stared at his crumpled face.

'Happy birthday! You've grown beauteously! I haven't seen you since you were a little baby. What a calamity that was… you know you almost got away from us.'

'Thanks but I'm Lydia, not Livia.'

'Ah same difference, tomato, toma-toh.'

He put his handkerchief in his breast pocket and ruffled her hair. After Lydia cleaned herself up in the bathroom she headed to the dining room. All of the guests were gathered around the table. She waded through the multitude of guests and stood beside her sister. They both smiled as everyone took pictures.

Their mother soon entered holding a cake with eight candles lit. 'First we'll open the presents, then we'll proceed to cut the cake.' She placed it down on the table. 'Go on Livia, you go first.'

This year was no aberration and Lydia had accustomed herself to the status quo. Whilst cutting the cake - their mother would recount Livia's childbirth. Followed by everyone raising their glasses in admiration. Often, their mother would embellish the tale and make it much more death defying, and without fail Aunt Ophelia would roll her eyes and down a glass of gin.

'Thank you everyone for the lovely gifts, I'm very grateful,' said Livia and she moved aside so Lydia could open hers.

'Oh Onata that cake looks mighty delish!' yelled a voice in the room.

'It's a divine walnut cake with all the trimmings, I had the baker make it from scratch,' she replied.

As Lydia opened her gifts, Livia scooped some of the cake onto her little finger and tasted it.

'Wow what a wonderful encyclopedia set!'

'What about my doll's house?'

'Maybe next year sweetheart,' said the mother.

All of a sudden Livia started to cough uncontrollably.

'Livia what's wrong?'

But she was unable to respond and her face turned red like a tomato.

'Heavens she's choking!' cried the mother.

One of the guests barged past Lydia and knocked her off the chair. He attempted the Heimlich maneuver but Livia's condition only worsened and her eyes turned bloodshot. Lydia hid behind her aunt in fright. 'Somebody call an ambulance!' yelled another guest.

Medics soon arrived and rushed Livia to the hospital. After a short examination they discovered the cake triggered a nut allergy and she was fortunate to have received medical attention so efficiently.

*

Time soon flew and the girls found themselves in middle school. Livia always pipped Lydia by the post on averages, and she was adored among the teachers.

The week before summer vacation both girls were placed in the final of the school's annual spelling bee. It was an illustrious event, billed like a boxing match – sister vs sister - with the winner receiving a cash check worth $1000, and their name engraved on the library plaque. Livia studied all week long and didn't concern herself with distractions from the school and local media.

The big day arrived and both girls battled through a host of elongated words. At the three hour mark Livia was finally crowned champion, as Lydia stumbled on the Latin word 'Invidia.'

Back at the house the family threw a grandiose celebratory party for Livia. Various family members and guests fawned over her, and Lydia was forced to watch her sister glisten in the limelight.

That night Lydia entertained thoughts of hurting

her sister, either by secretly adding nuts to her food or even smothering her with a pillow. But she couldn't bring herself to it. While Livia was giving a speech to the guests, Lydia crept out of the house and snuck into Aunt Ophelia's apartment down the road.

When her aunt returned home inebriated she found her niece crying on the bed. She flicked on the light and sat next to her. 'Lydia? What's the matter?'

She didn't respond and her aunt dried her tears.

'Does your mother know you're here? Everyone must be worried sick.'

'Everyone loves Livia, no one cares about me!'

'Lydia that's not true, we love you both equally.'

She wrapped her arms around her niece and held her tight. 'You know I must be honest with you darling, I know exactly how you feel.'

'How?'

'Well something tells me history is repeating itself. Every time I look at you, I see myself and every time I look at Livia I see my sister.'

'Mother?'

'Yes my dear.'

It went silent and Lydia gazed around her aunt's room. There was a large makeup table with a vanity mirror and on its surface were various bottles of alcohol and an ashtray. Framed posters of actresses from Hollywood's golden age were also scattered around.

'I know all too well about living in the shadow of a sibling. Lydia and your mother were born lucky. But don't let them tread on your dreams. You can be anything you want to be.'

Lydia sat up and her aunt brushed her hair.

'I'm going to teach you a magical phrase, a phrase that's helped me through dark times.'

'What is it?' asked Lydia curiously.

She held her niece's hand tight.

'Someday my time will come.'

'Someday… my time will come,' copied Lydia.

'Say it again.'

'Someday my time will come.'

'That's my girl. Now whenever you feel like your sister, your mother or the world is getting the better of you, repeat it to yourself and believe it will hold true.'

*

From that day forward whenever Lydia felt insecurity conjure inside of her, she repeated her trusty phrase – 'Someday my time will come' and like magic all of her troubles would disappear.

Lydia and Livia soon grew into beautiful teenagers. In their final year of high school, Lydia found herself competing with her sister again, but this time for boys as well as grades.

On Valentines Day Lydia set her sights on James. He was a sweet boy who was very handsome and like most students in their school – he came from a wealthy background. Deep down his heart cried for both of them and not wanting to upset one twin over the other he decided to ask both of them out. Lydia upon receiving his invitation was excited at first, but not wanting to appear needy she waited a few days before messaging him. Livia on the other hand called him post-haste and scheduled a date. They hit it off immediately and soon became a loving couple.

'Someday my time will come,' whispered Lydia as she watched her sister drive off in James's car one Friday evening.

'He's such a sweet boy. I'm so happy for my Livia. What about you Lydia? Any boys you have your eye on?' asked the mother as they sat down for dinner. Lydia stumbled for words and Aunt Ophelia sensed her niece was stressed from the probing.

'Well sometimes I guess you have to kiss a few frogs before you find your prince,' she interrupted.

Lydia just smiled and tucked into her sea urchin.

*

The first few months of college proved interesting. Livia was distraught, as she and James had peacefully called time on their relationship due to their respective busy schedules. But one fateful day her luck soon changed, as she was offered a full scholarship into Harvard medical school. She had entered a taxi and made pleasant conversation with a fellow passenger, who turned out to be a professor. He admired her diligence and offered her a grant the very next day. When Lydia heard the news, she brushed it off as another moment of sheer luck.

Lydia who always saw herself as the modest twin, was also accepted into Harvard, but unfortunately she never received a scholarship and was forced to pay the gargantuan tuition fees. She was envious at first, but her special phrase eased the pain.

Due to both sisters studying different subjects, the fierce competition was removed from the equation. Lydia found solace in this, and excelled in advancing her career as a lawyer. Livia on the contrary found the never-ending workload of becoming a dental surgeon a drudgery. Nevertheless she persisted and completed her assignments to the best of her ability.

Five years later, the pendulum finally swung in Lydia's favor and her phrase started to bear fruit. She landed a lucrative job at a prestigious law firm, whereas Livia was having a hard time working menial jobs. At the family dinners every other month, Lydia couldn't help but deservedly gloat. 'So how's the waitressing job? Do you get good tips?'

'It's not ideal, but you get some high profile clients every once in a while.'

'You have good grades, why don't you just a get a real job for the time being?'

'Because I want to be my own boss and work for myself not someone else.'

'I still think you should get a proper job.'

'Lydia, I've told you dozens of times. You must always think long term.'

'Well you can always come and work for me. I could do with an assistant,' muttered Lydia.

*

As the months went by Lydia advanced to the top of her law firm and was given a promotion to be made partner. Elated beyond belief, she rung her sister to break the good news.

'Oh Livia you'll never guess what happened!'

'Lydia I'm so glad you called, I have some terrible news… mother died in her sleep.'

Hundreds of people turned up to the mother's

funeral. The mother's body was enclosed in a white coffin and one of her requests before parting was to redirect money spent on floral arrangements to the local hospice. It was a bright summers day and the twins stood atop her grave in matching black dresses. Aunt Ophelia wore her expensive fur coat and crystal hung from her earlobes. Their mother's death wrenched Livia's heart and between the two, she cried the longest and hardest.

Weeks after the funeral, both daughters received a lucrative sum of money from their inheritance. Livia chose to invest the capital in her business, whereas Lydia decided to spend it on a lavish six-month vacation. She needed time to relax, especially after all her tumultuous hours at work. She knew she had a cushion of a well-paid job so she made sure to stay in the best places money could buy. Not wanting to appear inconsiderate, she sent Livia a "Wish you were here" card every time she reached a new destination.

*

When Lydia returned home she discovered Livia had successfully established her dental practice. As she opened her mail that evening she nearly coughed up her heart. The letter stated that her law firm had gone bankrupt and she'd been made redundant. Lydia once again felt her world crumble, and now destitute, she was forced to sell her apartment and move in with Aunt Ophelia. Her aunt even sold her lavish fur coat that she loved dearly so she could aid her financially. Lydia against her wishes took a job as receptionist at her sister's dental surgery.

As the months passed, Lydia desperately searched for a new job. She hated working for her sister and as a result she increased the repetitions of her phrase to fifty times a day and even recorded herself and listened to it while she slept.

Finally one October morning she awoke to news of a successful job application at another law firm. She rung her sister post-haste to celebrate the news.

'Livia I finally got...'

'I was just about to call you,' she interrupted.

Her voice tinged with a sorrow cadence. 'Are you sitting down?' asked Livia. 'It's just... Aunt Ophelia passed away last night.'

Lydia upon hearing the news, fainted.

*

The twins counted just three others at their aunt's funeral service. It was a murky morning and the smell of rain made the occasion sour.

'It's such a shame she's gone. If only she gave up the drinking and smoking sooner,' lamented Livia as she threw a clump of dirt into the hole.

Lydia ignored her sister's remarks and stood in sorrow until the priest made the sign of the cross.

Everyone left the cemetery and both twins stood disheartened. 'I know this is neither the time nor the place, but whatever money we receive from Ophelia I'd suggest spending it wisely. It was always her wish to see you prosper,' added Livia.

Lydia glared back at her. The wind disturbed a black feather mounted on her hat and the rain made a river of her mascara.

'How dare you?!'

'What?'

'Who are you to tell me what to do with my money!' yelled Lydia.

'I didn't mean any harm in it, it's just…'

'All my life I've been in your shadow and you've loved every minute of it! Aunt Ophelia was the only one who cared about me!'

'Where is this coming from?'

'You just cant help yourself can you! Always telling me what to do. Well no more, it ends today!'

'Lydia what do you mean?' she asked shocked.

'Someday my time will come… That time is right now!'

She flung off her hat and stared at her sister one last time.

'I'm leaving for good! You'll never see me again.'

And with that, Lydia cast off her sister's mental shackles and walked onto the road without looking back or looking at all. She heard Livia scream but she ignored her. At long last Lydia was finally free. Her life flashed before her and she recalled all the torment and harsh comparisons. She stared at the gray clouds in the sky and as her eyes closed, she whispered her favorite phrase over and over.

'Someday my time will come… Someday my time will come…'

*

A few days later, the phrase *'Someday my time will come.'* was engraved into an expensive marble gravestone paid for by her sister Livia.

Careless Talk Costs Time

When it rains, it pours and when it pours the deity of any city is its taxi driver. Demarcus sat in his warm air-conditioned cab, watching Manhattan's mask of fortitude disintegrate in the rain.

Pedestrians with umbrellas packed the sidewalks. Some ran for shelter whilst others shielded themselves with newspapers. The silver spoons of the Upper East Side shuddered in disdain as they shared the same rainfall as the homeless and the hookers.

With the flick of a switch the taxi's availability light glowed. Akin to dropping blood in a shark tank, it attracted the attention of many. A businessman clawed his way to the front of the pack and opened the door. The relentless sound of sirens and shouting pierced the warm serenity. Raindrops pelted the leather seats and the man's bony fingers grasped the handle and shut the door. Demarcus focused on melodious pitter-patter of rain hitting the windshield.

'Listen buddy I'm running late! If you can get me to JFK airport in twenty minutes I'll double the fare.'

Demarcus strapped his seatbelt and peered over the seat. He scanned him like a tailor eyeing a man for a suit. 'Sir you might wanna buckle up, and you see that little handrail - hold on to that too.'

The man slowly fastened his seatbelt. Demarcus waited for him to hold the handrail but he declined. Demarcus turned back to the wheel.

'Have it your way.'

He twisted the keys and the engine ignited. The traffic lights flashed green and Demarcus slammed the gas. The businessman slammed back into his seat like a rag-doll as the cab blasted through the wet metropolis.

'I've been a cabbie for ten years. Some say I'm the best in the business, some say the best in New York, hell a few argue I'm the best in the East Coast! Truth be told, all I care about is getting from A to B.'

Demarcus tapped the meter, which hadn't even hit $2:00. 'My service is better than the subway. And unlike other drivers I make most of my capital in gratuity or in cases like yours - double or nothing.'

The man nervously glanced at his watch.

'No need to clock watch sir!'

The speedometer needle smacked sixty and the cab effortlessly weaved through the multitude of vehicles.

'The secret to being a good cabbie is knowing your client. Don't be a wallflower but don't talk too much either. If you want to maximize your tips you have to steer the conversation to the customer. You can't expect the Upper East Side wives to break bread if you talk to them like the flash boys of Wall Street. Just agree to all their remarks and throw in a compliment about their sequined blazer or diamond earrings. Whereas the suits, you just remain stoic and get them from A to B. It's also best to collect them after their power-lunch, they'll be high as a kite and they usually tip higher.'

Passing traffic blurred past as the cab jetted down the Long Island expressway.

'What about the bums and junkies, you ever give them rides?' asked the man.

'Sure I don't discriminate. They never give me any trouble and I don't expect them to tip. After all they don't live in the Hamptons.'

The cab suddenly jolted right.

'Come on! I'm running out of time!'

'We're on the home stretch sir. Just keep talking. A watched pot never boils.'

The man remained silent and stared at the overcast sky from the window.

'You got any kids?' asked Demarcus.

'Nope, waste of time. You?'

'Got a little girl, she's turning five in a few days time. What about a lady? Fine man like yourself should have a dime piece back home right?'

'Nope, once again waste of time… and money.'

'I actually met my girlfriend of seven years in this very cab. I was driving down the Queensboro Bridge and I saw this chick on the side of the road. Her car had broke down so I picked her up, pro-bono. She was going on a date and was wearing this fine-ass dress. So, I worked my charm and when she was on her date… apparently I was all she could think about.'

'Wow… lucky you.'

'Not luck sir, I'm always in pole position, that's why they call me the blitz. Demarcus 'The Blitz' Blake. Has a nice ring to it don't you think?

The clouds above the car whooshed past and a low flying aircraft ascended in the distance. Demarcus skidded into terminal five and charged towards the entrance.

'What? How did you know my terminal?!'

'This is chess not checkers sir, I'm always ten steps ahead.'

Demarcus slid into an empty parking bay yards from the entrance. He checked his rearview and noticed the man's knuckles had turned white. The man threw some cash onto the seat and quickly exited. Demarcus unwound the window and laughed as he dashed frantically to the entrance.

'You're welcome!'

He smiled as a $100 bill danced on the breeze above the seat.

*

Demarcus counted his tips under the light from a streetlamp. The sidewalks were deserted and his boss's voice scratched through the intercom.

'Demarcus… it's almost midnight.'

'Punching out now boss.'

He pocketed his tips and turned off the duty light. The wind howled and the stained glass windows from a church glinted the moon's reflection. Demarcus drove ahead and noticed a man in a trench coat standing on the sidewalk. He drove slowly and tried to make eye contact, but his face was concealed under the shade of a fedora hat. The man glanced towards the cab. He departed with his cigarette and hailed for the cab. Demarcus considered leaving him but it was too cold of a night.

'I guess one more ride can't hurt,' he muttered.

Demarcus flicked on the duty light and the man strolled towards the cab. As the man edged closer, he pulled something from his pocket. Demarcus gripped the wheel tight. The man ripped open the backdoor and hurried inside. 'Park Central Hotel please.'

Demarcus locked his gaze on the rearview and tried to discern what he was clutching. The sound of a dialing tone destroyed the tension and the man put a cellphone to his ear. Demarcus laughed softly and drove off into the night.

The man was courteous compared to most passengers, but everything about him just seemed odd. As the car moved under the various streetlamps Demarcus occasionally peered into the mirror and studied him. He was wearing a suit cravat with smoke grey trousers and his shoes were heavily polished like tiny black mirrors. It was like he'd stepped out from the 1920s. His call finally connected and Demarcus deftly eavesdropped.

'I've been trying to reach you for days… Funny how every time I lend you money you develop amnesia!'

He spoke with a thick New York accent and constantly gestured with his free hand.

'That's Mr. Darl to you… don't feign ignorance with me, I was just at the church sorting out your former boss's funeral arrangements.'

Demarcus looked at him through the rearview but this time Mr. Darl made eye contact with him. Demarcus quickly averted his gaze and stared back to the road. Mr. Darl lowered his voice significantly so Demarcus covertly switched off the intercom.

'We've gone over this plenty of times! When I pull out my gun that's your cue. Don't miss it like last time.'

Demarcus's fingers gripped the wheel tight.

'Why did I pick up this lunatic?' He mumbled.

'What'd you mean you're nervous? So what if there's a big crowd?'

The cab stopped at a set of traffic lights and Mr. Darl abruptly opened the door.

'Just keep your mouth shut and be there! The big day is at the end of this month… you'll know because I'll be wearing my navy suit.'

He cut the call and hastily exited the cab. He buried his chin under his coat and walked away. Demarcus rolled down the window. Just as he went to speak - Mr. Darl paused and turned around.

'Sorry, where are my manners?'

He took out a wad of cash and threw a $20 bill onto the seat. Demarcus stared in confusion as the man disappeared through the foliage of Central Park.

*

The following afternoon was crisp and chilly. Waning sunlight broke through the clouds and forced Demarcus to drop the sun visor. He took a bite from his sandwich and checked his voicemail.

"Hey babe, you barely said a word last night. Is everything okay? Anyway I made you a sandwich in the fridge. I know you love eating out but I just figured with a baby on the way we should be saving. Call me when you can. I love you."

Demarcus opened the glove compartment and pulled out a family photo. As he smiled in the pleasant memory, someone unexpectedly entered his cab. 'Sparks Steakhouse please. East 46th Street.'

Demarcus peered over his shoulder and scrunched his face. When he realized it was Mr. Darl he almost chocked on his sandwich. He was on the phone again but this time he had a laptop. Demarcus quickly turned around like he'd seen a ghost.

'Of all the cabs in the city what are the chances?' he thought.

Mr. Darl fastened his seatbelt and yelled down the phone. 'You're saying it all wrong, say it again!'

Demarcus now ever more keen on investigating, continued to eavesdrop.

'He's gonna get whacked today. I don't give two shits if it gets messy... Just make sure it's quick and bullets don't go flying.'

Demarcus bit his fingernails and glanced in the wing mirror. The cold light of day exposed Mr. Darl's features. His face was small but oily, and the skin around his eyes was stretched backwards like he'd been involved in some sort of accident. His mouth, even if it wasn't moving carried an expression of distaste.

The road ahead was clear but Demarcus purposely veered into the traffic so he could keep listening. Mr. Darl suddenly opened the door and scurried out.

'Driver I'm gonna grab a paper.'

Demarcus remained still.

'I have to keep the meter running.'

'Relax, I'm good for it.'

There was a line at the vending machine and with the traffic ahead not moving. Demarcus quickly unbuckled his seatbelt and slithered into the back. He clawed at the laptop with fingers, but as he spun it around, the traffic lights turned green. True to the New York minute - the cars behind beeped violently. Mr. Darl approached the cab with a newspaper in hand. Demarcus hurriedly scrolled down the page and realized it was a schedule. He swiftly took out his phone and took a picture. He frantically closed the laptop and spun it back around. The cars behind continued to honk and Mr. Darl entered the cab.

'Funny I don't remember shutting the laptop?'

In the corner of his eye Demarcus sensed Mr. Darl scanning him, but he remained calm and kept his hands on the wheel.

Mr. Darl shook his head and sat back down. Demarcus sighed in relief and drove towards the steakhouse. As they parked up, Mr. Darl's inflection turned vitriolic.

'I'm gonna drop by the Triangle club around midnight. I can't wait to bow over his dead body.'

Mr. Darl dropped another $20 bill onto the seat and exited. Before pulling away, Demarcus watched from afar, as two men in expensive suits greeted him.

*

Night fell over Manhattan and Demarcus ventured into the cab depot. Drivers waxed their cabs and the smell of gasoline was rife. His boss yelled over the clanking sounds of metal.

'There's the blitz!'

'Listen Phil, can we talk in private?'

'Sure… right this way.'

Demarcus took a seat in his office. A dusty PC sat on a table full of stacked papers. His boss sat opposite him and fiddled with a replica toy taxi.

'So what's up?'

Demarcus considered telling him about Mr. Darl but had second thoughts. There was no way his boss would have believed him.

'Come on blitz you didn't drag me in here for nothing did you?'

'Is it possible I could get some overtime? Maybe do a few graveyard shifts?'

His boss leaned back in his chair and grinned.

'Christ that's all you wanted? What's with all the dramatics? You know I'm always looking for more drivers. When'd you wanna start?'

'Tonight.'

'Wow what's brought this on?'

'Family sir, me and Lana… we got a little one on the way, so every little helps you know.'

'Well congratulations blitz! Yeah to hell with it, you can start tonight sure. I'm working too so it'll be just like old times.'

Demarcus tried to smile authentically. His boss

leapt up and hurried to the door.

'Anyway I have a meeting. Keep up the hard work.'

Once he'd left, Demarcus slammed the door and closed the blinds. He foraged through his desk and concealed under some pay slips was a Glock-19. He made sure it was loaded and gazed at his employee of the year photo on the adjacent wall. He took a deep breath and buried the gun in his pocket.

*

Demarcus parked in the shadows opposite the Triangle Club. It was approaching 11:30PM. He hid the gun under the seat and sweat dripped from his forehead. His phone vibrated and sent shockwaves over the cab. He left it to voicemail and his wife's voice echoed.

'Sorry to hear you have to do overtime. Drive safe. I love you.'

The lights inside the club switched off and a Black Mercedes pulled up outside the door.

Demarcus leaned forwards and crouched under the steering wheel. 'What the fuck?'

Two shady men dashed inside and the car screeched and took off. Demarcus quickly grabbed his phone and dialed 911.

'911 What's your emergency?'

'There's been a shooting, or something bad has happened! The Triangle Social Club.'

'What's your name sir?'

'Demarcus 'the bli… Demarcus Blake!'

'Sir I need you to stay on the phone with me, are

you alright?'

'I'm just a cabbie. Get here quick!'

Demarcus cut the call. He was breathing so hard the windows had turned foggy. A cop car soon pulled up and two armed officers knocked on the club door. No answer. Demarcus watched as they crept into the alleyway. They soon returned with their guns in their holsters. One of the cops spotted the cab and marched over. Demarcus unwound the window. The cop had a face like a python and scowled at him.

'Are you the one who made the distress call?'

'Yes.'

'Did you actually see a shooting take place?'

'Well no, but...'

'Did you see any armed suspects?'

'No... but...'

'Did you see ANY CRIME take place?'

'No sir.'

The cop swore under his breath and spoke into his radio. 'Confirm, no ambulance needed.'

He gave Demarcus a fowl look. 'Do this again and we'll bust you for wasting police time.'

Demarcus slammed his fist on the wheel and buried his face in his hands.

*

Three days passed and although knowing Mr. Darl's schedule, Demarcus couldn't track him. He hadn't slept since the incident and his obsession with Mr. Darl was affecting his focus.

After dropping off a few passengers Demarcus decided to wait outside Mr. Darl's hotel. His phone rung and he answered.

'Hey.'

'Don't hey me Demarcus! You've been acting real strange lately. I know that you finish early today so don't pull some slick shit and come home late! In fact, at three o' clock - you can pick your daughter up from school, and then you can get something to eat, because I sure as hell ain't cooking for you!'

She hung up before he could even reply. With thirty minutes to spare he decided to drive back to the Triangle club – hoping he'd find Mr. Darl.

He parked the car out front and clasped the gun from under the seat. He stepped out of the cab and headed towards the alleyway. An open drain spewed a vile stench of sewage and he scrunched his face. The floor showed no signs of blood, so he checked the dumpsters for any foul play, but to no avail.

The backdoor of the club flew open and two men wearing tracksuits stormed out. One wielded a baseball bat, and the other had a Saint Anthony tattoo on his bulging forearm.

'Who are you?!'

Demarcus quickly backtracked down the alley.

'I said, who the fuck are you?'

He sprinted back to his cab but in the scramble he dropped the gun. He scrammed inside the cab and saw the two men pick up the gun. He started the engine and rocketed away.

'Listen I'm gonna be a bit late, the driver's just got in the car now.'

Demarcus jumped in fright and slammed his head against the car roof. He peered around. Mr. Darl was sitting in the back of the cab. He took his ear away from the phone. 'Park Central Hotel pronto.'

Demarcus took a longer than average route to elongate the conversation again.

'How was I supposed to know he'd show up at the club two hours early? Either way my guys took care of him.'

Demarcus berated himself silently.

'Don't worry, I've had time to practice my speech. The guy's hogged my limelight for too long… Yep that's right - Sparks Steakhouse – Friday 9PM.'

Demarcus pulled into the hotel and watched Mr. Darl walk into the lobby. As Demarcus scooped the cash from the seat, his heart sunk as he realized the time. He slammed the gas and sped to the school.

*

Demarcus was unshaven and his eye bags were so heavy they appeared to weigh down his face. He sighed as his boss removed his employee of the year photo. 'Don't give me that look Demarcus! Twenty complaints lodged in the space of three days! What are you playing at?'

'Sorry Phil, just with the baby…'

'No excuses! You were fine when Chloe was born, in fact I remember your service was at an all time high back then.'

'So what happens now?' asked Demarcus

'You're on graveyard shifts from here on out. Hopefully the passengers will be too drunk to complain.'

Demarcus shook his head and stared blankly at the clock on the wall. It was fast approaching 9:00PM and all he could think about was exposing Mr. Darl. His boss was still talking but he wasn't listening. His boss slammed the table.

'See this is what I'm talking about, your attention span is worse than a fucking fish. The other guys always give me grief because I always give you the benefit of the doubt. Well no more. Last warning, any more incidents and you're suspended!'

'Phil it won't happen again, I promise.'

*

Passing traffic whizzed by as he sped to the steakhouse. He swerved into an empty parking spot and took out his phone. He polished the camera and started recording as he entered the steakhouse.

It was dimly lit with small tables covered in red and white tablecloth. New York's infamous history was soaked into walls, with pictures of Al Capone and the Five Points Gang. Demarcus curled into a leather booth and veiled his face behind a menu. He scanned the restaurant for Mr. Darl, but as usual he was nowhere in sight.

A young waiter approached the table and Demarcus shooed him away. He looked at his watch – it had just gone 9:30PM and the only people in the restaurant were a family of four.

'Where the hell is he?'

A large shadow suddenly engulfed the table and the candle blew out. Demarcus hesitantly peered up and spotted the two men from the alley. They seized him by the neck and dragged him through the kitchen and out into the alley.

He wheezed in pain as they slammed him to the wall. They both took turns punching him in the face. Blood dappled onto his shirt and one of them ripped it open. 'No wires.'

He brandished the gun Demarcus dropped days prior. 'Isn't this yours? Tell me now what you're doing here!'

'I'm looking for Darl! Mr. Darl.'

'Darl, I dunno any Mr. Darl.'

Demarcus spat out blood.

'Please I have a kid! I have a little girl.'

'That's nice, whaddya think she prefers, open or closed casket?'

The man cocked the gun and jammed it between Demarcus' eyes.

'Please, I just came here looking for a Mr. Darl! I'm not police, I'm just a cabbie! This is a big mistake!'

The man looked to his partner who just shrugged his shoulders and pulled a face.

'Listen I dunno who you are, or who this Darl guy is, but if I ever see you here again we'll put you in a body bag and throw you in the fucking Hudson River.'

He loosened his grip and took away the gun. Suddenly he fired a shot and shattered the cab's taillight. Demarcus flinched as he shoved the gun back to him.

*

As Demarcus drove back, a cop car forced him to pull over. A cop tapped his window with a flashlight.

Demarcus' bloodshot eyes dilated in the narrow beam.

'Look who it is, the cabbie who cried wolf.'

Demarcus looked up confused and realized it was the same python-faced cop.

'License and registration.'

Demarcus reluctantly handed them over.

'I swear to god there must be over eight million people in this damn city! My luck I keep running into the same ones,' he muttered.

The cop returned and threw back his papers.

'Your taillight is out. Your cab is unsafe to drive.'

Demarcus puffed.

'I was just about to let you off, but I didn't like the tone of your puff. So here's a lovely ticket courtesy of the NYPD. You have a nice night now.'

*

'Wasn't it just a few hours ago that you promised me shit like this wouldn't happen again?!'

'Sorry boss, it's just…'

'I don't wanna hear it! That taillight's coming out of your wages. And what the fuck happened to your face? I'm well within my rights to fire you Demarcus, but out of respect for who you once were I'm gonna let you off. As off right now… you're suspended! Go clean out your cab.'

Demarcus sat silently in his cab. He called his wife but it diverted to a pre-recorded message.

"I've moved back into my mom's apartment. Forgetting your daughter at school was the last straw. And if I find out you've been cheating on me, we're finished!”

Demarcus dropped the phone and battered the steering wheel with his fists. Blood trickled down the side of his face and he slid the gun into his mouth. His hands trembled and he desperately wanted to pull the trigger, but something caught his eye. Underneath the gas pedal was a scrunched family photo. He clasped it and burst into tears. He pressed the photo to his heart and closed his eyes in the darkness of the cab.

*

Two weeks passed and Demarcus returned to his cab. The last light of day crept behind the skyscrapers, and he'd just dropped off another passenger in record time. The passenger handed him a crisp $20 bill. His boss mumbled through the intercom. ‘Good to have you back blitz.’

‘Good to be back!’

‘Has your wife forgiven you yet?’

‘Well she told me to call her tonight. So I'm gonna give her the most sincerest of apologies.’

Demarcus dropped off a few more passengers and switched off the duty light. He took a deep breath and called his wife. After a few rings - she answered.

‘Hey Lana, how are you?’

‘I'm doing okay.’

‘And Chloe?’

‘She's fine… We miss you Demarcus. She wants to come home… so do I.’

‘I've missed you both too. I just want to tell you how sorr…’

Suddenly someone entered his cab.

'West 51st Street please.'

Demarcus lowered the phone and looked in the rearview. It was Mr. Darl. He noticed Mr. Darl's distinct navy suit and remembered it was his big day.

'Lana I'll call you back! Sorry I love you!'

Demarcus threw the phone onto the seat and accelerated. His heart pounded rapidly and he discreetly started recording on his phone. Mr. Darl was on the phone, but this time he was also holding a small booklet. 'It's finally the big day! Come on don't sound so nervous, we've practiced this a hundred times.'

His intonation was far softer and Demarcus bit his tongue, confused.

'Make sure you drink some warm water - it's great for your vocal chords… Speaking of that, I should hang up, I don't want my throat getting dry. Break a leg!'

He cut the call and straightened his tie.

Demarcus pulled up. Mr. Darl exited and scurried to the driver window. He handed over a $20 bill and smiled.

'You know, I feel like I've seen you somewhere before, please do keep the change.'

He scurried off into the bustling crowds. Demarcus scrunched his face and exited the cab dumbfounded. He dashed into the hoards of tourists and pedestrians but couldn't pinpoint Mr. Darl. Unremitting, Demarcus continued his search and squinted under the bright lights of Broadway

Under The Moonlight She Flourishes

Captain Jack Redsky and his unit ducked from the onslaught of enemy gunfire. The scent of death gusted the air whilst debris and smoke whipped their faces. Redsky hurled a grenade over the wall. A deafening blast shattered their eardrums and the opposition gunfire ceased.

'Move out boys! Chambers will cover us!'

They sprinted inside the building and Chambers sniped the surrounding soldiers. The helicopter blades above sliced the air and augmented the commotion.

'Shit! Where's Leffen?!' yelled Spector.

Redsky peered from the window and spotted Cadet

Leffen still on the battlefield. 'I'll go back and get him! You get on the chopper now!'

Redsky dashed back into the warzone. Leffen was crouched beside his former partner. The soldiers steel dog tags were decorated in blood. Redsky shook his head in dismay.

'Leffen we have to move out now!'

An enemy soldier appeared from the carnage. A distinct scar on his left eye trickled all the way down to the corner of his mouth and he fired at close range. Redsky leapt and pushed Leffen to safety. The bullet ripped into his shoulder. He dropped to the floor and thudded to the dirt.

~

Jack awoke in fright and squinted at the noisy air-con in the hotel room. He'd fallen prey to a recurring nightmare. In the mirror he glared at the scar on his shoulder and rubbed it with his cold hands. He withdrew a photo of his wife and daughter and stared through it. His facial muscles fought but couldn't yield his bitter resentment. Jack scrunched the photo and threw it into the bin.

He put on a white shirt and a navy blazer then clipped a war medal onto the lapel. He buried his hand into his pocket and pulled out a diamond engagement ring. He took a deep breath.

'Laura will you marry me… Laura Lima, will you take my hand in… Laura I love you, will you marry me…' A noise from the bathroom shook him and he quickly concealed the ring in his pocket. He crept towards the door and peered in. Mist from the shower caressed his stubble and the smell of apricot shampoo whiffed as his girlfriend washed her hair.

His phone rung, so he quickly closed the door. Jack stared at the number hesitantly and cut the call. He quickly raided the wardrobe and found a bed sheet. He knelt under the bed and covered a war-torn black briefcase with it.

They were staying on the tenth floor and he stared out the windows. The view overlooked the city - Jack with his gaze of cold command - stood akin to a lone wolf - stalking the campfires of unwary travellers.

He opened the large window until the safety lock jammed in. Dismayed, he withdrew his pocketknife and shoved it into the hinge but it wouldn't budge. The shower ceased and Jack quickly closed the window and switched on the TV. His girlfriend emerged from the bathroom drying her hair. Her feet left moist patches on the red carpet.

'What's the weather going to be like?' she asked.

His phone rung loudly and Laura winced.

'Aren't you gonna answer that?'

'No.'

'What are you up to?' she asked smiling

He cut the call and turned back to the TV. The weather displayed signs of gusty winds. He clenched his teeth and his face turned red.

'Are you sure this was the only room available?'

'I told you, it was the best the company could do at such short notice.'

She slipped off her towel and threw it on the bed. Jack scooped it up and hung it over a chair. He ran his hands over her slender body and kissed the top of her shoulders. Her skin was moon white and she had dark hair that he loved to grab and pull. Laura took her black sequined dress from the closet. Jack's eyebrows contorted. 'You don't like it?'

'I'd prefer if you wear the red one. Tonight's our anniversary. I want you to stand out from the crowd.'

'You haven't even told me where we're going?'

'It's a surprise. Now put on the red dress. That's an order,' he said with a grin.

She smacked his chest and smiled. 'Yes captain.'

His phone rung and he stared at it reluctantly.

'I'm gonna take this outside.'

Jack exited the room. He walked to the end of the hallway and answered the call. 'Listen, it was the best I could do… just do your fucking job! You'll get what's owed to you once I have the money.'

*

Laura scanned the huge marble foyer and headed to the toilet. Jack made his way to the reception but none of the staff were available. He repeatedly slammed the bell until a clerk arrived.

'The windows in my room don't fully open. Do you have any balcony suites available for upgrade?'

'Can I have your room number sir?'

'Room 851 – 10th floor.'

Jack watched him as he typed into the computer like a courtroom stenographer.

'Ah Mr. Redskee?'

'Redsky.'

'I'm sorry sir?'

'I said it's Redsky. You know, like the untouchable 'sky' that's always above your head and can rain down on you whenever it pleases.'

The man, ambivalent to his rebuff just smiled.

'My apologies Mr. Redsky. Yes I can see here you're booked under your partner's name, Laura Lima. Hotel regulations state - any windows on floors seven and higher must be equipped with a safety lock.' Jack clenched his fist and stared up to the crystalline chandelier.

'Fine, hand me a spare room key.'

'Give me one moment sir.' He ducked under the counter and produced another room key card. Jack concealed it in his pocket.

'Is there anything else I can help you with sir?'

'Yes. What's the quickest way to get to the restaurant from here?'

'Which one sir? There are dozens of Michelin starred restaurants around the area.'

'I forget the name… Beyond The Luna?'

The man delicately smiled.

'Something funny?'

'I think you mean *Quantum Ad Luna*.'

'My apologies. I didn't major in Latin, I was too busy protecting this country.'

'Just turn left from the entrance and head straight, you won't miss it.'

'You can't miss what?' interrupted Laura.

'You're stealthy for a women in heels,' said Jack surprised.

'Is there anything else I can help you with sir?'

'Negative.' Jack walked away and put his arm on the small of Laura's back.

'Please tell me where you're taking me?'

'That's twice you've asked,' he said with a smile. 'Do it again and I'll dismiss you for insubordination.'

As they walked towards the restaurant something made Jack halt. Sitting down next to a phone booth was a homeless veteran. He had a leg missing and his dog tags were concealed under an antiquated grey coat. Jack glared at his wounds and trembled. Laura knelt and handed the veteran a $20 bill.

'My Jack also served. He still suffers from PTSD. Please take this.'

Laura put the money in his hand and clasped it shut. The veteran mumbled his generosity. Laura rejoined Jack and together they walked off. A cold wind tore through the evening and Jack suddenly walked back to the veteran. Laura watched in the distance as Jack spoke to him and shook his hand. When he returned, he put his arm around her and smiled.

'Hopefully he'll get a room for the night.'

Laura kissed him and held him tight.'

'That's very sweet of you.'

'Let's just enjoy the rest of the evening,' he added.

*

The balcony of Quantum Ad Luna was only accessible by special reservation. A tall security guard who matched Jack for height only let him pass once he'd given his name. They rode the glass elevator to the top of the tower and it automatically stopped on the correct floor. The smell of wine and grilled meat wafted through the air. A man wearing a black blazer with the restaurant crest over its pocket approached them. He forced a smile to appear on his face. 'Good evening sir, thank you for choosing to dine at Quantum Ad Luna.

He grabbed two menus and led them outside. They reached the balcony and Jack surveyed the area. A small orchestra played live music and a circular bar served cocktails in the foreground. All the men wore suits and every woman had on elegant eveningwear.

Their table was next to the balcony and Laura gasped at the view - which overlooked the skyline.

'A waitress will be with you shortly,' said the host as he walked off.

Jack held her hand. 'The reason what makes this place so special is the view, and when there's a full moon it illuminates the entire balcony. But not only is today our anniversary, it's also the day of the super moon.'

Laura screamed in excitement and kissed him everywhere she could. 'This is the best anniversary gift ever,' said Laura as she pointed to various sights. 'Look you can even see our hotel room.'

Jack guided her into her seat and sat down. He broke a piece of bread into two halves and ate one. Laura just ate a few olives and swayed to the music.

Jack abruptly stood. The screech of his chair made Laura and some of the guests shiver.

'I need to use the bathroom.'

'Now? What if the waitress comes over?'

'Just get my usual.'

'Scotch?'

'No, not tonight. Just water please.'

'Really?'

'For now, please... I won't be long.'

Jack flashed a fictitious smile and entered the

toilet. He checked the stalls to make sure they were empty and manically splashed cold water over his face. He pulled out a scrunched document from his blazer pocket and stared languidly in the mirror. His eyes scanned the page and he started reading out loud.

'Jack Redsky, due to your inconceivable actions… it is with immediate effect that you are dismissed with disgrace.'

Jack's breathing intensified and he ripped the document to pieces. He scrambled into a stall and locked the door. A hot flush spilled through his body and he clamped his eyes shut.

~

Redsky awoke in a hospital bed. The first thing he saw was Spector and Chambers by his bedside. A heart monitor beeped rapidly. He sat upright and tried to piece together his fragmented memory.

'Where am I? What happened?'

'Welcome back Red!' said Chambers.

Spector grabbed his hand and squeezed it.

'Good to have you back captain.'

He looked down at his hospital gown and inspected the medical instruments attached to his body. 'You were shot on the battlefield and fell into a coma,' added Spector.

'How long was I out?'

'Three months.'

Jack looked around crestfallen. There were flowers all around his bedside and sympathy cards were scattered around the table.

'What the fuck is all this?'

Spector and Chambers suddenly stood with

sorrowful faces. 'I don't know how to break this to you captain...'

Redsky waited for them to fill the silence.

'While you were unconscious... Back home your wife and daughter were involved in a car accident. They were rushed to hospital, but sadly they both passed... I'm so sorry captain.'

Redsky stared despondent and watched the air con waft a trio of helium balloons.

'Thank you soldiers. You're relieved.'

'Captain if there's anything we...'

'You're relieved...'

*

Two years passed and Redsky rejoined his infantry. A crescent moon crept behind the vanilla domed mosques as the Humvee drove through the barren streets.

'Good to have you back Captain!'

'Good to be back Lieutenant.' He rotated his right shoulder in small circles and eyed the pair of them.

Redsky switched off the headlights and veered into the sand.

'Captain the barrack is back south,' added Chambers.

'I know it's short notice, but I need you to accompany me on a little side quest,' said Redsky.

Spector's face contorted and he peered over from the passenger seat. 'What are you talking about?'

'I was just briefed by the colonel about a secret initiative. There's an abandoned house a few miles from one of our active warzones. We have reason to believe some form of terrorist activity is occurring there. I need you to help me survey the area.'

'Yes sir,' said Chambers.

They pulled up yards from a barbed wire enclosure and got out of the car. Redsky withdrew some wire cutters and opened a gaping hole in the fence. Spector and Chambers cautiously examined their surroundings. It was extremely dark and their GPS systems were unworkable.

'Something about this doesn't feel right,' added Chambers.

'I'm with you on that one,' said Spector.

Redsky stood on the fence to stop it from swaying in the wind. 'After you gentlemen.'

Spector and Chambers took a deep breath and squirmed through the fence. A sinister look took hold of Redsky's face as he checked his weapons.

~

Jack stumbled back to the balcony, it was dark and flaming torches were lit around. He stared nervously at his watch. It was 10PM and he set a timer for midnight. He spotted Laura in the red dress.

'Where have you been?!' she asked.

'Sorry,' said Jack as he gulped his glass of water. Laura noticed he was sweating but blamed it on the fiery torches. After they'd finished eating. Jack stared out towards the sky. The moonlight broke through Laura's hair and she rubbed his knuckles with her finger.

'Jack let's talk about…'

'Laura I love you. Remember I quit the marines

so we could be together. I've never said this until now, but I want to settle down with you, maybe even start a family.'

Her eyes filled with tears and she rummaged inside her handbag. Jack took a swig of water and focused on her intently.

'That's the first time you've said you loved me.' She put some papers on the table and took out a fountain pen. 'I think we should do the right thing. I've been considering this for some time now, and if we really want to think about kids we have to secure ourselves. At the shareholders meeting earlier, I found out our stock has skyrocketed since that other pharmaceutical company went into liquidation. And since my father passed, I pretty much own the company now.'

Jack continued to glare at her.

'I want you to sign this contract. God forbid anything happen to me, the assets of the business will be bequeathed onto you.

He grabbed the pen and stared intensely over the balcony.

'Thank you Laura. I love you,' said Jack and he signed the papers.

'I know we're meant for each other,' she added.

Laura finished her glass of wine and excused herself. 'Gosh I'm so excited, I need to use the bathroom!' She kissed him and skipped off.

Jack watched her leave and glanced at his watch. Midnight was fast approaching and he dabbed his sweat with a napkin. Unexpectedly another hot flush surged through his body. He drank down Laura's wine and groaned in discomfort.

~

They crouched behind a muddy bank and peered outward hesitantly. Spector surveyed the area with his night vision binoculars.

'Tell me what you see.' ordered Redsky.

'There's a dozen small houses. One of them has two men by the door.'

'That's the one,' snapped Redsky.

Childish laughter and giggling echoed lightly.

'What was that?' asked Chambers.

'Shit, there's two children playing on the terrain.'

Redsky grinned and cocked his gun.

'Follow me boys.'

Chambers blocked him with his arm.

'Captain does anyone even know we're here?'

Redsky scowled. 'Listen to me very carefully. If you help me out on this, I'll make sure you both get a Medal of Honor. Now move out.'

Redsky leapt over the hill and ran through the mud. A rupture of light flashed from his rifle. The shot obliterated one guards face. Screams reverberated from the houses and the two children ran inside towards their mother's screams.

The second guard spotted them and opened fire.

'Shit! Take cover!' yelled Spector.

Spector covered him whilst he reloaded. Chambers sniped the remaining guard and Redsky dashed towards the house. Spector and Chambers covered him by the window.

Redsky kicked the door off its hinges. An unarmed man shielded his wife and children. Redsky marched over and slammed his fist into the man's scarred face.

'Remember me?!' he screamed. 'Because of you, my wife and daughter are dead!'

He battered his face with the gun and cracked his teeth off the marble floor. His blood splattered the walls and stained the light bulb. Spector dashed inside and snatched Redsky's rifle.

'Captain we have to leave now!'

Redsky ignored him, but the man escaped with his family through the backdoor.

'Shit!' Redsky lunged after him and gave chase.

Chambers closed in on him. Redsky, with no firearm rashly grabbed a grenade from his belt.

'No! Captain don't do it!' screamed Spector.

Redsky ignored his pleas and ripped off the pin. He launched the grenade. Spector yelled for everyone to take cover but it was too late. A seismic bang ripped apart the ground and a miasma of smoke engulfed the area. Shrapnel and debris lashed their faces, and the pebbled ground became lubricated with blood. Redsky panted and smiled. Spector clutched his bloodied face and limped over to inspect Chambers. Redsky trudged over and his face turned white. Chamber's leg had been blown off. He screamed in agony and they dragged him to the Humvee.

~

Jack felt a cold tissue on his forehead and woke up in a shock. Everyone in the restaurant stared at him with upturned faces and Laura poured him some more water. 'What's the matter?'

The wind gusted the balcony and Jack buttoned his

blazer making sure the signed contract was secure in his pocket. 'I'm fine, let's just enjoy what's left of our anniversary.'

The large vanilla moon adorned the balcony in its luminescence. Jack and Laura slow danced to the mellow music of the orchestra. He glanced at his watch and realized it was almost midnight.

'So where's this surprise that you've been teasing me with all night?'

Jack pulled her towards his chest and kissed her. When he finally let go, he stared at the stars reflected in her eyes, and they somehow lost their radiance. Jack took her hand and led her up some steps and onto a small circle, which was coated in moonlight.

A waitress in the foreground held a bottle of champagne and all of the guests glared in wonderment. He cut the timer on his watch and knelt down on one knee. She gasped, and Jack brandished an engagement ring.

'Laura will you marry me?'

He waited for a response and a cold wind bit through the air. Laura let out a tiny scream, with a subtle cadence that seemed to distress the stars. She flourished under the moonlight and Jack gazed at her once beautiful red dress, which now seemed much darker under the harsh light of the moon.

The Man Who Followed Himself

Once upon a time in a city far away there was a young boy named Ethan. He was nice, well mannered, and like most young children he loved adventure. He was a prodigious artist and would spend hours sketching and painting the most exquisite pictures. Teachers and scholars fawned over his work, and many predicted he would brush shoulders with the crème de la crème of artistry.

But one rather unfortunate day, all of this changed - akin to smearing black paint over a canvas, Ethan's dreams of adventure and becoming an artist died. This all occurred on one peculiar day, the day Ethan decided to grow up.

During high school, peer pressure forced him to partake in subjects he had no inclinations for. He excelled in those areas, and as time passed he chiseled his creativity until it eventually turned to dust. However there was one subject Ethan truly adored, he could never understand it, nor put it into context, but he felt a visceral connection to it. Anytime he thought of this subject his heart would beat faster. This particular subject, was women. Oh how he loved women, their smiles, their curves, their nuanced graces, their complexity, their depth, but most of all… he loved their beauty.

But although Ethan loved women, he was hopeless with them. They were like butterflies that would flutter past, and he'd try his best to snatch them, but he never quite could, and eventually the wind would gust them away.

When Ethan came of age, he settled for a job with a small desk in a large office. Still the paragon of a soft-spoken nice guy, he would do various favors for his colleagues and bosses, hoping that one day they'd praise him for his generosity, but of course, they never did.

One evening Ethan finished his work and peered around the office. It was very male dominated and polluted with printers and computers. Amidst the noises of typing and phone chatter, he glared at his desk ornament – a ship inside a small glass bottle, which he'd constructed. He closed his eyes and imagined himself by the ocean, listening to the waves lap the shore.

Suddenly something crashed onto his desk and he awoke in fright. 'This will definitely keep your eyes open,' said his boss.

Ethan stared at his desk. His eyes could barely reach the summit of fresh paperwork.

'You want me to type up all of this?'

'Yes, why what's wrong?'

'Nothing… it's just, this isn't my work.'

'Ethan do you remember what I told you last year? If you keep going the extra mile, I'll put in a good word with the fat cats upstairs.'

Ethan pondered his claim and sat upright.

'How long do I have to keep doing this for?'

'Only time will tell, but it's the way of the world kiddo, sometimes you gotta shovel shit before you can see the garden.'

His boss walked away with a wry smile and Ethan watched as him and his colleagues put on their coats.

'Where are you going?'

'Ethan it's Friday night, the boys and me are going out for some well deserved drinks. Come and join us when you're done!'

*

By the time Ethan finished the mountain of paperwork he could see the stars from the window. He sighed as he turned off the lights and locked up. Feeling exhausted he was in no mood to get intoxicated, yet he headed to the bar anyway.

'Ethan you're gonna be swimming in money since you did all that overtime! The least you can do is buy everyone a round of drinks!'

He complied as usual and kept everyone happy. As the night went on, they ran up a huge bill and all left in secrecy, leaving Ethan to pay the lion's share.

Sitting alone with a drink in hand, Ethan examined his life. He thought about pulling his savings and going travelling. He was sick of the infested rat race and climbing the ever-sinking corporate ladder. He yearned to broaden his horizons.

Just as he was about to down his drink, something captivated his attention. Framed in the doorway against the light from outside was a female silhouette. She walked towards the bar and sat beside him. He remained indifferent and scanned her in his peripheral gaze. She wore a black dress, which failed to hide her curves and blonde hair cascaded down to the small of her back. She ordered a drink with a mellow voice and burst into tears.

'What's wrong?' he asked.

She looked up and her mascara trickled through her face like watercolor. Ethan pushed forward a napkin and she dabbed her tears.

'Thanks. I wish you hadn't seen me like this.'

Her breath smelt of cigarettes but he didn't mind.

'No you look beautiful, what happened?'

'I caught my now ex-boyfriend fooling around with one of my friends.'

'Sorry to hear.'

She smiled and Ethan bought her another drink. They talked for hours and he listened to her endless stories of heartbreak. Ethan berated all the other men that had wronged her and she quickly took a liking to him. At the end of the night Ethan walked her home and plucked up the courage to ask for her number.

Adriana wrote her number on the back of a napkin and put it in his pocket. She kissed him on the cheek and skipped to the door. Ethan stared at the napkin under the street lamp and felt a warm feeling flourish inside of him. That night he was so excited he didn't sleep a wink.

*

Months passed and with Adriana now the focus of his life Ethan decided to put his plans of travelling aside. He'd finally met a woman who gave him some reciprocation and he didn't want to curtail his chances. Ethan felt himself falling in love with Adriana. Above all, he was kind to her and he genuinely cared for her. He always complimented her, and he always commented when she did small things like change the style of her hair, because he was nice like that.

He often took her to lavish restaurants and he always made sure to pay the exorbitant bill. He was the guy after all and he was nice like that. A multitude of Ethan's friends warned him she was just using him, but he dismissed their terrible thoughts with jealousy.

Ethan's reward for his niceness was a monumental amount of teasing and flirting. She'd bestow him with hugs and kisses, sometimes even on the lips, but never too much, just enough to keep the carrot in front of the donkey. However, none of this bothered Ethan. He was resilient and he knew if he stayed patient Adriana would realize he was 'the one' and they'd live happily ever after.

One summer's day at the mall, Ethan was late for their coffee date – a usual thing every other Saturday.

As he waded past the hoards of people he noticed a newly opened art gallery. He walked on past but something compelled him to look back. He stared at his watch and sighed. Adriana had been late many times for their dates and at times she'd even cancelled at the last minute. After a few seconds of pondering, Ethan decided it wouldn't hurt his chances if he arrived late.

He peered into the gallery windows and felt something spark inside of him. There were glorious paintings of - mountains, forests, and his personal favorite - boats sailing at sea. He felt a strong urge to enter but just as he stepped inside, a familiar voice cried his name. It was Adriana.

He scurried over to her. She was standing outside the coffee shop and her face was scrunched.

'Ethan I've been waiting here for ten minutes!'

'Sorry… Find a seat and I'll buy the coffee?'

After Ethan purchased their drinks he scanned the area to see where Adriana was sitting. When he finally spotted her, his legs went weak. Not from adoration, but because he saw her exchange numbers with another guy.

When they finished their drinks, Adriana led him to the window of a jewelry store. She pressed her index finger on the glass and pointed to an opulent opal pearl. Her eyes glistened with hope and she squeezed his hand gently. 'If someone ever bought me that I'd promise to love them forever.'

Ethan, still depressed from earlier, quickly masqueraded a smile.

*

That very night after Ethan dropped her home, he drove up a steep bank, which overlooked the city. The sky was shrouded in a purple hue and he reflected upon his unfruitful relationship. He knew he had to win Adriana's heart. He had to flourish something so outlandish, it would separate him from the crowd. But what and how? He remained in deep thought until an idea flashed into his mind. He sat up elated. He knew this grand gesture would skyrocket their magical future. He grinned from ear to ear and sped back to the mall.

Ethan withdrew a huge amount of money from a cash machine and headed to the jewelry store.

It was moments from closing and Ethan dashed to the entrance.

'How much for the pearl?!' he panted.

'$1000,' said the manager.

'Please I have $900 right here in my hand.'

'Sorry no can do.'

The man continued to close the shop. Ethan sighed and pressed his face onto the cold glass.

'It is real pearl right?'

'That thing? No, but it's the closest thing to real you'll ever find around here.'

'No... It has to be real. Where can I find a real pearl?'

The man closed his shop and walked away laughing. 'In the ocean!'

Ethan trudged off dejected. He walked past the art gallery and stared into the window. Once again the paintings of oceans and opalescent vistas stirred something in his heart. Finally, it struck him. He would seek out a real pearl from the heart of the sea. He would travel far and wide and retrieve this rare pearl, then present it to Adriana as a symbol for his unremitting love. He wanted Adriana to hear of his courage, and hardship that would be enmeshed in an arduous journey. The more he thought about it, the more he knew he had to go.

So the next day Ethan packed a small bundle of provisions, quit his job, and without telling a soul, he left in the middle of the night on a journey to the far and distant sea.

*

After enduring three long bus rides and hopping two freight trains, Ethan arrived at a rural village at the foot of a large mountain. His hair was windswept and stubble had gathered around his usually smooth face. He searched his pockets for his trusty map but in horror, he realized he'd left it on the bus.

Ethan scoured the village looking to purchase a new map or guide. He looked everywhere but unfortunately he couldn't communicate efficiently with the locals. At dusk, he came upon a tiny market stall run by an adolescent boy. Ethan noticed he was selling various hiking equipment. 'Excuse me, do you know where I can find a map?'

The boy stared at him in confusion.

'I need a map, because I want to climb the mountain,' added Ethan.

He laid some cash on the table. The boy took the money and counted it.

'This is too much money,' he said.

'You speak English!?'

'Yes. I learnt from my parents.'

'Where are your parents?'

'They died long ago on the mountain... This is why I make a living selling mountain equipment.'

'I'm sorry to hear, well I'm sure they would be proud of you... So do you have a map I can buy?'

Again the boy glared at him strangely. 'Why are you climbing the mountain?'

'What do you mean?' asked Ethan surprised.

'Why do you wish to climb this mountain?'

Ethan explained his story about Adriana and the boy stared at him profusely.

'I've seen many travellers faces. None of them have looked as frightful as you. This quest, it is noble, but it is also a hole. A hole that you desperately seek to fill. There is only one thing that must be done... you must be thrown into the hole.'

Ethan shook his head in confusion. 'So you do have a map for me?'

The boy smiled. 'I will give you a place to stay for a few days. You can shower, eat, and experience the village. I will not take your money, but you must help me set up and close the stall each day. I think you will learn and experience many things. Only when I think you are ready for the mountain, will I give you a map.'

Ethan looked up at the towering mountaintop. Simply thinking of the ascent left him downbeat, but he thought of Adriana, and reminisced about her smile. Her spirit revitalized him and he immediately shook his hand.

*

The boy's name was Ram, and Ethan stayed with him for two whole weeks. During his tenure Ethan accustomed to a new way of living, and experienced the wonders of life without technology and noise. Every night the villagers would gather around the fire and trade stories of the day. Ethan loved this, and he shared many stories about Adriana, art, and his love for the sea.

When Ram decided Ethan was ready, he returned with a map for him. 'Take it and go in search for the treasure you seek. I know in my heart that you will find much more.'

Ethan thanked him profusely and headed for the mountain.

*

Snow fell endlessly and the path to the summit was enveloped in treacherous black ice. Ethan's hands were frostbitten and he hadn't eaten in days. Half way up the trail Ethan stumbled upon a small cafe that doubled as a lodge. Almost on the verge of fainting, he decided to retire for the night.

He warmed his hands by the fire and in the foreground he spotted a waitress. She had a few iridescent tattoos and her wrists were covered in rope bracelets. Crimson hair swooped over her eyes and there was something alluring about her. She smiled at him and came over. 'Have some of this,' she said and handed him warm mug.

Ethan stared at the drink dumbfounded.

'Relax, it's just hot chocolate,' she joked.

Ethan smiled and took a sip. 'Thank you.'

'So are you scaling the mountain?'

'Wow how'd you know?'

'Well that big backpack kinda gives it away.'

They both laughed and Ethan noticed her eyes closed when she chuckled. She sat down opposite him. 'My name's Farin by the way.'

'I'm Ethan, nice to meet you,' he said and he shook her hand.

'So what brings a good boy from the city to a daring place like this?'

'I need to get my girlfriend a rare pearl. So I've travelled all the way here to get to the sea.'

'That's sweet, how long have you been together?'

'Well she's not really my girlfriend... yet.'

Farin scrunched her face and evened it with a smile. 'Well I'm sure she'll admire your spirit of adventure... I sure as hell do.'

'Thanks... so what about you?'

'My grandparent's own this lodge so whenever I need money for travelling I work a few shifts here and there.'

'Where are you heading to next?'

'I'm gonna go diving in the Great Barrier Reef.'

Ethan sat up and his chair and leaned in.

'I've always wanted to do that too! I love boats and the sea.'

'Nothing makes me feel more alive than travelling. Since we're living in this huge world, we should do our best to experience every inch of it.'

'I couldn't agree more.'

'Well maybe we should travel together? I leave in

a few months if you're around?'

Ethan smirked and felt a tingling sensation swirl inside him. He stirred his hot chocolate and stared at the brown whirlpool. 'I'd love too, but first, I must get the pearl… It's just something I have to do.'

Ethan paid the bill and left her a nice tip.

'It was nice meeting you Ethan. I hope our paths cross again,' said Farin and she handed him a receipt.

She smiled at him one more time as Ethan headed to one of the vacant rooms.

Before he fell asleep, he looked at the back of his receipt and noticed Farin had wrote down her number along with a smiley face. He grinned and closed his eyes in the warmth of the cabin. The next day Ethan scaled the hazardous mountain. As the falling debris battered his face he thought of Adriana, and how he missed holding her hand. Eventually he ascended and ultimately reached the summit.

*

At the base of the mountain Ethan arrived at a brooding forest. His hands and knees were bloodied and the torrential rain only made things worse. Under the dark elms, he aimlessly traversed in circles and became hopelessly lost for many days.

It was well past midnight by the time he found habitation and it was in the form of a noisy cabin-bar. Pick up trucks and motorcycles were parked around its entrance and he walked inside slowly.

Shivering and covered in mud he waded to the bar. It was gloomy and the head-splitting music battered his ears. He managed to order a glass of water but the barkeep just gave him a tankard full of beer. As he searched for an empty seat the partygoers constantly pushed him from side to side. By the time he'd sat down his glass was half empty. He laughed to himself and closed his eyes in the commotion.

*

When Ethan opened his eyes he sat up hastily. There was a large muscular man sat opposite him. He had long black hair and his biceps were as big as bowling balls. His left eye was forever squinted and scratches and scars etched his cheekbones. 'If someone bought me a beer every time I received that look from strangers… I'd be the happiest man alive.'

'What happened to you?' asked Ethan

'Life.'

'What do you mean?'

'That's the problem with you pretty boys, you ask too much questions.'

Ethan clamped his mouth shut and stared out the window.

'Come on! I didn't mean no harm in it! What I'm tryna say is, if you keep asking life small questions, you're only gonna get small answers.'

The man watched Ethan struggle to invent the perfect question and laughed.

'What's your name kid?'

'Ethan.'

'I'm Sage.'

The man shook his hand extremely hard and Ethan tried not to squirm.

'Why are you here Ethan?'

'I'm trying to get a woman to like me.'

'So you came to a bar full of loud, overbearing, sweaty men?'

Ethan laughed and sipped his beer. 'I'm on my way to the sea. I want to get her a rare pearl.'

'See right there, that's a small question… I'm tryna get a woman to like me.'

'What do you mean?'

'I've learnt a lotta things in my time and the size of your problems will always be the size of your life. Instead of asking - how can I get a woman to like me? You should be asking. How can I become a man who women desire?'

Sage watched Ethan ponder his question and he ordered them another round of drinks. When he returned Ethan was sat up smiling. 'Judge a man by his questions not by his answers!'

'There you go, that's exactly my point!'

'What else can you teach me?' he asked.

'Seems to me like you're learning along the way… I don't know how long you've been on this journey, quite frankly I don't care, but the most important thing is you're willing to get your hands dirty. When you're faced with a fork in the road, always take the path that will give you the best memories.'

Ethan stared at the smudge-marked glass and reminisced his journey. Everything Sage said struck a chord inside of him.

*

Light poured in from the window and lit the mahogany table. Ethan awoke and thought the meeting with Sage had been a dream. Confused, he hurried outside but all the vehicles were gone. White sunlight broke through the branches and last night's rainfall dripped from the foliage. He glanced at a sign that detailed the harbor was a few miles south.

He ran as fast as he could and soon he saw the sea. Finally, after all the hazardous and tribulations he found himself near the sea. The seagulls cawed and the salt-tinged wind splashed mist over his cheeks. Ethan felt broken and battered but somehow the sea restored him. It was everything he'd imagined. Wasting no time he sought out the fishermen by the harbor.

'Excuse me gentlemen but I've travelled from far away… I'm here to seek out a treasure, a luxurious pearl for a woman I love.'

In unison they scrunched their wind burned faces and laughed. Some suggested a few souvenir shops but Ethan remained adamant that it wouldn't suffice. With no help, he walked along the shore downcast and considered his options. Suddenly he heard a voice call his name. A fisherman with a harpoon approached him. 'To seek a natural pearl is a challenge, but you may borrow my boat!'

Ethan hugged the man in excitement. 'Thank you! But why are you helping me?'

'A man passed through the harbor early this morning. A kind man who I'm indebted to. He mentioned you and told me to help in any way I can.'

Ethan smiled and thought of Sage. Without hesitation he hopped into the fisherman's boat and sailed off to the heart of the sea.

*

After three days battling with an unforgiving storm- swept sea, Ethan was ready to give up. He was exhausted and his low food supplies had left him tremendously weak. But he thought of Adriana, and imagined her kissing him when she received the beauteous pearl. So Ethan exchanged blows with nature once more. Gray clouds and lightning gathered above. Waves licked the boat and it almost capsized. Still he battled and fought, and finally he managed to grasp a natural pearl. The rain lashed his face and he held it close to his heart. At last with the pearl in his possession he set sail back to shore.

*

Finally Ethan arrived back home, battered, bruised and scarred all over. He took a much-needed shower, combed his hair, put on his favourite shirt, and arranged for Adriana to meet him on the beach.

In the glorious sunset Ethan waited for her near the shoreline. She arrived fifteen minutes late but nonetheless she was thoroughly surprised to see him. For he had been gone for such a long time and she was even more amazed when he recounted his adventure. He spoke of his hardships and told her about the village, the mountain, the forest, and he told her about the sea. Mostly he told her about the sea.

And so, at long last, Ethan stood tall before her, and with great flourish, displayed the exquisite pearl. Her face lit up like the stars at night and she wept and fell into his arms. She proclaimed then and there she would love no other man but him.

'No one has ever done something so beautiful for me!' she cried. 'Most men are such creeps... Like this guy that I met a few weeks ago... Oh and by the way I have to see him tonight. I think he's just using me, so I'm going to set him straight. But don't worry because now I finally know what I want. So tomorrow I'll call you and we'll make plans, or maybe the day after, but definitely sometime this week. Most of all thanks so much for this gift, you're so amazing!'

However as she embraced him tightly, Ethan found himself looking over her shoulder and towards the distant horizon.

She smiled at him and he thought of the village.

She held his hand and he thought of the mountain.

She kissed his cheek and he thought of the sea... Most of all he thought of the sea...

So Ethan placed the pearl in her hand and walked away.

A Woman's Work Is Never Done

Every morning in accordance to the rising sun, Heather Harper would wake up and prepare herself for a rigorous routine of housework. The first thing she would do was slip on her tortoise glasses and read not the morning paper, not a book, but her never-failing notepad. It was a container for all her chores - complimenting a schedule that was airtight and often penned the night before. It would be impossible to find Heather without her notepad; she held it like a weapon and safeguarded it akin to a dog with a bone.

She had an oval face with long brown hair. However, she would only let it down in the evening. During the day it would always be tied back with not a strand out of place. Her hands were always soft with sanitizer and they forever smelt of washing up liquid or bleach.

She had a penchant for floral dresses, in fact her entire wardrobe consisted of them. She had a dress for every day of the week and she even coordinated them to every season. Heather also took it upon herself to sew small pocket squares into them - to secure her trusty notepad.

Heather considers herself a perfectionist and frowns upon spontaneity. Whenever she changes a light bulb, she always records the date so she can plan accordingly and not be left in the dark so to speak. She always uses a saucer when drinking tea and she spends more time washing the TV than watching it. The bed would be off limits once made, which meant no hanky panky whatsoever. That time had to be reserved and would only be granted if her schedule allowed.

Heather shunned those who disbelieved in the archetypal housewife, and she blamed society for the death of the Renaissance woman. She bestowed a rather dry sense of humor and most of her enjoyment, if not from cleaning, derived from crossword puzzles and trimming the garden hedges into animals.

As it was springtime, Heather arose early and slipped on a blue flowery ensemble. She then made herself a detoxifying honey and lemon ice tea - to cleanse her body whilst she cleansed the homestead. A regular day would be to; prepare breakfast, clean the kitchen, vacuum the carpet, dust the corners, clean the bathroom, water the flowers, prepare lunch, clean the kitchen, mow the lawn, prepare dinner, clean the kitchen, clean the bathroom, then finally go to sleep but not before penciling in tomorrow's schedule.

Her husband, Ken Harper was a quite a botchy man who often wore slacks with braces that did nothing to stop his stomach spilling over his waistline. He was past retirement and spent most of his time at the country club. He also worked there voluntarily as he hated being stuck in the house with his wife. Ken was apathetic to Heather's regimented routine. Every year she would buy him day socks and become angst when he didn't wear them on their appropriate day. More often than not he was the root cause of her anal-retentive behavior. He always knocked things over in heavy-handed fashion and never used a coaster when drinking beverages. However, although Heather would never admit it, Ken making a mess was an aphrodisiac to her – as it would always lead to more housework.

'Why can't we get a dog?' asked Ken one evening. 'Bill at the club has a beautiful German Shepard, keeps him and his wife great company. I think it could do us some good. You know, spice things up.'

'Absolutely not! A canine in the house would represent anarchy and I for one will not be scooping up excrement from the carpet. Heavens no, just think of all the fur that would lodge itself inside the sofa.'

'That's why they call it fur-niture love,' added Ken with a grin.

'Absolutely not!'

*

The next day Heather found herself in the garden exactly on schedule. The sun shone brightly and she daintily watered her Lilies of the Valley.

'Sweet day ain't it?'

Heather looked up and glared at Mrs. Holland's face, which was planted on the wooden fence. It was round and had the familiarity of a cabbage. A polka dot scarf pulled her hair back and although it was a forty-degree day she still wore a grandiose fur coat.

'Heavens, aren't you boiling?' asked Heather. 'It is a lovely coat though!'

'Isn't it just! Snagged it for a great price too as one of the neighbors was selling it dirt cheap.'

Heather put down her watering can and walked towards her. Mrs. Holland took off her sunglasses and allowed the sun to warm her crow's feet.

'Oh Heather, it breaks my little heart to see you work so hard. Let me find you a nice housemaid. Women our age should enjoy these years!'

Mrs. Holland's mouth had a predilection for moving in a manner in which it had no control of what it was saying. Since her husband left, she had nothing better to do than pamper herself all day whilst her three housemaids did all the work.

'That's sweet of you, but I like to do everything myself. You know my saying. A woman's work is never done!'

Mrs. Holland sighed and popped a straw into her mouth. 'Whatever you say Heather dear!'

Beyond the fence Heather heard the rattling of ice cubes clattering against crystal and she caught the scent of vodka as Mrs. Holland slurped it through the straw. 'How's Ken by the way?'

This was another trait that Heather despised, as Mrs. Holland was always flirtatious with Ken.

'He's at the country club I imagine,' she scoffed.

'I often see him working up a sweat on the golf course. I'd love for him to show me his swing some time... do tell him I said hello.'

Heather smiled and walked back inside. Mrs. Holland bellowed from over the fence.

'Oh! I almost forgot! Heather would you be a dear and lend me that lovely purple dress of yours?'

Normally Heather hated lending out her dresses, but seeing as she was falling behind schedule, she quickly headed upstairs and fetched it for her. Heather never exercised as she burned hundreds of calories a day simply by cleaning, whereas Mrs. Holland's monthly liposuction was the only reason they shared the same dress size.

'Don't worry, I'll return it and have one of my maids dry clean it for you.'

'No! Please don't, I'll wash it myself thank you.'

'Now I won't keep you any longer from your "spring cleaning."'

Heather bit her tongue. She hated those two words and considered them blasphemous.

*

Heather and Ken's silver jubilee anniversary was fast approaching and as the days ran together, Heather noticed Ken was spending an abundant time at work and the country club. After numerous wasted dinners, Heather decided to confront him. 'Where in heavens have you been?!' she demanded as he strolled in past ten in the evening.

'I told you, I've been playing extra games with

Bill down at the country club.'

'Well I've just spoken to Bill's wife, and she told me hasn't played golf since he dislocated his shoulder a month ago. So where have you been!?'

Ken's face turned pink and he marched into the kitchen. He threw cold water over his cheeks and reheated a plate of chicken in the microwave.

'Stop ignoring me! Where have you been?'

'Okay… I've been doing overtime. I wanted the extra money to buy a new set of clubs. I knew if I told you, you'd say no.'

Heather wiped away her sweat.

'Next time you must tell me what time you're coming home so I can make a note! I can't live a life not knowing what to expect around every corner!'

Over the course of the next few days Ken continued to come home late. With her suspicions further aroused, she called up his work and discovered his story was fabricated.

One evening, whilst he ate in the kitchen, Heather scoured his pockets for any clues but found nothing. But upon holding his jacket to her nose she picked up the aroma of perfume. It smelt familiar and she stayed awake all night pondering the scent.

That very evening Heather switched off the house lights, and waited like a snake in the grass for Ken to emerge. At nine o'clock sharp, headlights from his car passed over the curtains and she glared from her shady vantage point. He leapt from the car with a spring in his step and whistled a tune. However instead of coming home he trotted around the fence and entered Mrs. Holland's back door.

Heather scrambled outside and clambered over the

fence. She crept behind the bushes and patiently waited. It didn't take long for Mrs. Holland to wander into her living room wearing her purple floral dress. Much to her horror, Ken soon appeared holding a lustrous diamond necklace. He wrapped his arms around her fat neck and clipped it on. Heather seethed in anger and watched as Mrs. Holland twirled in a circle, blowing imaginary kisses like a cheap Marylyn Monroe.

Back home Heather untied her apron and flung it over a chair. She sat under a dim light in the kitchen and glared at her Lilies of the Valley. She drank white wine straight from the bottle and a scornful vengeance began to take hold. With each passing second, Heather's animosity built. Then at exactly midnight, it erupted in cold calculating fashion.

*

It was the day of their silver jubilee anniversary and Heather arose bright and early with a demeanor that radiated devil may care. She slipped on a black floral dress and carefully slid her notepad inside the breast pocket. She finished all her chores in record time and even managed another cheeky glass of wine.

Ken arrived home early and greeted her with a kiss. 'Happy anniversary my love.'

Heather simply smiled and continued to chop the carrots with her favorite knife.

'I'm cooking a succulent meal with all the trimmings. Go and watch the TV, I've left some saltine crackers for appetizers.'

Ken couldn't believe his luck and hurried into the

living room.

Heather soon called him when dinner was ready and he drooled at the delicious array of food. Ken quickly tucked in and Heather slowly watched him devour everything on the plate. After he'd finished eating she instructed him to lie down to correctly digest the meal. She dimmed the lights and violently increased the thermostat. He soon fell asleep in the humidity, and Heather quickly removed all but one of the liquids in the refrigerator - her homemade ice tea with extracts of Lilies of the Valley.

In the middle of the night Ken awoke with terrible hot flushes. He hurried downstairs, ripped open the fridge and gulped down half the bottle of ice tea. He wiped his mouth with his forearm and suddenly wheezed in agony. Dark blood spewed from his nostrils and he sneezed violently, spritzing blood all over the kitchen counter.

It was impossible for Heather not to hear his cries of pain and she watched from atop the stairs, as he crawled towards her begging for help. Bloody handprints enriched the maroon walls and pints of his blood seeped into the beige carpet. Heather just giggled and cheerfully kept adding to her to-do list. When he reached the top of the stairs, Heather dragged him to the bedroom. 'I know what you've been up to,' she whispered.

Ken grasped his neck and vomited the remnants of dinner all over the bed sheet. 'I saw you last night with that cow next door. To think you were fooling around the day before our anniversary!'

Ken shook his head and clawed at the bedposts. He tried his best to speak but the only thing that emitted was blood. Finally he let out a horrifying roar. His eyes rolled to the top of his head and he fell backwards - dead on the carpet.

As soon as the sun rose, Heather went straight to work on her gargantuan to-do list. First, she dragged his lifeless body into the kitchen. She considered cremating him, and using his ashes to make a hourglass, so Ken could finally help around the kitchen. But the more she pondered that course of action, she realized it was far too conspicuous. Instead, she dug a huge hole in the garden and flung Ken inside it. She then planted some flower seeds over the patch and vigorously watered them.

Heather spent the next two days cooped up inside the house, drastically cleaning and removing all shreds of evidence.

*

After a week of being a recluse, Heather became paranoid about hidden traces of blood. She wandered around with a magnifying glass and inspected every single nook and cranny of the household.

One night, after feeling weak and weary from all her cleaning, Heather retired rather early and fell asleep on the sofa. While she nodded nearly napping she heard a gentle tapping coming from the garden door. She awoke in a fright and peered through the purple curtains, but couldn't see anything except a raven pecking at the flower patch. She stepped outside and shoed it away. Suddenly she saw Mrs. Holland peering over the fence. She screamed into the night and fixed her nightgown.

'Didn't mean to scare you. Just I haven't seen you in a while,' said Mrs. Holland.

'You know me, a woman's work…'

'I know, I know, just I haven't seen Ken around either.'

Heather stared down at the flower patch. Her heart started to beat loudly and she cleared her throat.

'He's been sick this past week… must've been something he ate.'

'Poor thing, send him my love.'

Heather grinned and headed back inside.'

'That reminds me!' yelled Mrs. Holland. 'How was your silver jubilee? Ken told me all about it, he even let me model a diamond necklace he bought for you! Ain't you a lucky gal, having such a lovely husband willing to splash the cash.'

Heather's face turned cadaverous and without responding she hurried inside and slammed the door. She ran upstairs and searched frantically through Ken's belongings. However at the bottom of his sock drawer, she found a receipt detailing its worth for over $5000. Thinking about her huge mistake wrenched her heart and she vomited all over the bed sheets. That night, Heather crept into the garden and silently dug up Ken's body. Inside his trouser pocket she found the extravagant diamond necklace.

Over the next few days Heather cleaned the house to sheer perfection. Her once smooth hands now felt like sandpaper with the forceful rubbing. Yet no mater how hard Heather scrubbed, cleaned or dusted, she couldn't clean her mind of its mental cobwebs. Her once humble abode now harbored too many bad memories. Out of options, she sold the house – for a heavily reduced price.

Two weeks later, whilst Heather helped the removal men load her belongings into a van, Mrs. Holland approached her on the front lawn.

'Oh it pains me to see you leave so sudden.'

'I know, but with Ken relocating because of business it's for the best. It was nice knowing you Mrs. Holland. I'm sure we'll keep in touch.'

Just as Heather entered the taxi, Mrs. Holland bellowed out to her.

'That reminds me! Please do send me a postcard with your new address. I know you said not too, but I had your dress dry cleaned. I'll have it delivered as soon as I get it back sweetie!'

The cab drove away and Heather stared at her once lovely home and wished it a final farewell.

*

Heather acclimated to her new apartment well. It was spacious with a balcony and a glorious view that overlooked Central Park. She still hadn't unpacked and there were many boxes dispersed around.

She had just completed her afternoon shopping and was sweating abundantly as the elevator was out of order. It was incredibly hot for this time of year, and feeling parched, she scanned through her belongings for a drink. In one of the smaller boxes she found her infamous bottle of ice tea and placed it on the counter. She glared at it in remorse and compared it to Pandora's box. Beyond the counter, she noticed the red light blinking on her answer machine and hit play.

'Mrs. Holland here! Hope you and Ken are well. I miss you both... Oh that reminds me! The new neighbors are digging up the garden to install a hot tub! Perfect for this weather don't you say? I better get my swimsuit ready! Ciao!'

Heather's face turned crimson and her breathing became erratic. She hunted through her possessions and grasped her shovel. She scrambled to the door and as she flung it open, she spotted her neighbor's husband, Mr. Bell - who during the day worked as a deliveryman. Sweat dripped from his forehead like a waterfall and he stepped inside, holding a thin box.

'Hello Mrs. Harper,' he said panting. 'I have a dress I need you to sign for.'

'I'll have to sign for it later! Please make yourself at home!' yelled Heather as she slammed the door and dashed away.

Mr. Bell stared back in confusion and placed the package on the counter. He wiped away his sweat and poured himself a refreshing glass of ice tea.

A Most Unusual Day

The family didn't believe in quality time. It was the tail end of July and they were stuck in a car destined towards their vacation house. The sky was clear blue and the sun's rays amused themselves on the leathery seats. The father drove over a pothole and the mother smudged her lipstick across her lips.

'Why do we have to go on this stupid vacation every year? I'd be much better off alone at home,' said Sara, as she twirled her gum around her finger.

'We just do, besides the fresh air will do us all some good.' said the father.

Sara puffed and spat her gum underneath the seat. Her younger brother, Ryan, leaned over his mother's shoulder and peered out the window. Behind the red clay banks, he spotted a penitentiary enveloped in barbed wire fencing. 'Can we go and visit?! I've always wanted to meet a felon!'

'Don't be stupid,' muttered the father.

'I heard a killer recently escaped from that place.'

'You and your fables,' said the mother.

'I'm not lying! I heard it on the news!'

'I didn't hear nothing,' said the mother.

'That's coz all you do is watch the shopping channels,' he replied.

The car stopped outside a gas station. The father turned around and handed everyone some cash. The gas station was barren and the scorching sun baked the asphalt. Ryan and Sara breathed in the gas fumes. Their mother smacked them and ushered them inside. The cowbell above the door rung and Ryan and Sara dashed to the confectionary.

The owner was an old man with white hair, his cheeks were pink and he wore a lumberjack shirt that was tucked into his trousers. The father opened a packet of beef jerky and ate them on the way to the counter.

'Spending time with the family, that's nice' muttered the owner.

'Yep, we own a summer house down near the woodlands.' He peered behind and made sure his family had left. 'Truth is… I only come up here for the Indian casino. I use the kid's inheritance fund. They won't amount to much so I might as well use it on red or black.'

The owner tutted and rung up the items. As the father counted his cash, he noticed a wanted poster stuck on the window.

"Wanted dead or alive - Jacob "the spider" Sawyer - $5000 reward." No shit! So the boy weren't lying! What did the bastard do?'

'I heard they call him thc spider because he crawls into peoples homes and kills em while they sleep. Just a few days ago, local police found some dead bodies down in the badlands near some cactus. No evidence if it's that felon, but you know, no smoke without a fire.'

The father paid him for the goods and dropped a few cents into the tip-jar. 'If I win big at the casino, they'll be plenty more where that came from.'

*

They drove off into the hot afternoon and the kids sneered and emptied their pockets of stolen candy onto the seat. The mother turned around with a wry smile and shook her head. Twenty minutes later the car reeked of perspiration and was littered with confectionary. The father wound down the window.

'I'll give $10 to whoevers packet flies the farthest! Three, two, one – go!'

Everyone hurled their rubbish and gazed as it danced on the wind's breath.

'I won!' yelled Ryan.

'No mine's in the clouds!' screamed the mother.

'Not fair, you're at the front so you get more speed!' cried Sara.

'I won! Guess the $10 stays with me!'

The father put both of his hands back on the wheel. 'Global warming… fear mongering hogwash if you ask me. How is waste on the highway gonna lead to the polar ice caps melting? Besides, if we don't make a mess, how on earth will the cleaners get paid? It's the circle of life kids.'

Up ahead, a stationery police car started to flash its lights. A lone cop wearing a short-sleeved brown shirt and a wide brimmed hat waved them down.

'God damn pigs,' muttered the father.

'Afternoon sir, can I see your license and registration please?' asked the cop.

He handed them over and the cop glanced down without really paying attention.

'I'm officer Peyton Walker…'

Abruptly, the mother reached over and shook his hand. 'I'm Sienna,' she added pouting her lips.

'Nice to meet you ma'am. I hate to bother you on such a fine afternoon, but do you know the reason I pulled you over?'

'The litter?' murmured the father.

'Litter, what litter?'

'Nothin.'

'I pulled you over to inform you about the escaped convict.' He buried his hand in his pocket and handed them a wanted poster. 'Handsome fella!' yelled the mother.

Ryan leaned forwards and dug his knuckles into his mothers shoulders. 'See I told you! What he do? What he do!?'

Peyton sighed and glared at the sun.

'Oh come on! Spill the beans! Murder? Rape? Drugs? Grand larceny?'

Peyton wiped his sweat and spat on the floor.

'Well if any of you see him on the loose… my number's on the back of that poster.'

The wife put the poster in her handbag.

'If you see anything, don't hesitate to call me.'

'Anything to assist a man in uniform,' added the mother.

~

Peyton tilted his hat and banged the top of their dusty car with his palm. He took off his hat and sunglasses and sat in his car. He hadn't shaved in days and his eyes were bloodshot. He spat out the window and drove towards the gas station.

Peyton placed a six-pack of beer on the counter.

The storeowner raised his eyebrows.

'I'll give up drinking when my wife gives up her emotions,' said Peyton as he stuck a cigarette in his mouth.

'Any luck on catching that convict?'

'Jacob's been on the run for three days now. Bastard sure is one slippery serpent.'

He rung up his items and Peyton searched for his wallet. 'Shit must've left it in the car. Can you let me slide again? I'm still police after all.'

The owner sighed and handed over the items. Peyton helped himself to the tip-jar and grasped some coins. 'That reminds me - I gotta call the wife. Just put it on my tab.'

Peyton lit a cigarette near the gas pump and called his wife from the payphone. He took a long puff of smoke. Finally she answered.

'Hey babe it's me… I know, I know. Listen, I swear on our daughter's life I haven't touched any alcohol and I've given up the cigarettes… So can I come visit soon?' He stubbed his cigarette on the wall and crossed his fingers.

'Another month, sure… see ya then.'

Blood rushed to his face and he tore the phone from the line. He screamed violently and turned to the onlookers - watching him from their cars. He flicked his hair away from his face.

'Nothing to see here people! As you were!'

He gulped down a can of beer and flung it inside the dumpster. He lit another cigarette and sped off in rage.

~

A man emerged from the depths of the garbage and tossed aside Peyton's beer can. His green eyes adjusted to the sunlight and he clambered out and stretched. A tight-fitted denim shirt covered his skeletal frame and his ripped jeans and brown boots augmented his stowaway manner.

The gas station doors flung open and the cowbell broke off and rattled away. The man limped towards the counter and leered at the poster.

'Jesus Christ, I should have combed my hair.'

The owner looked up and stared at him. The air con fanned his dirty blonde hair and his coyote face matched the man in the poster. Sweat trickled from the owner's forehead.

'You're Jacob "the spider" Sawyer.'

'Well you're about as bright as the Louisiana sun.'

'Please, I don't have much money…' The owner's hands trembled and he pushed forward a pack of cigarettes. 'You can take these, all of them!'

'Cigarettes! I don't want no cigarettes. Those things kill people! Is that what you want, you want me to die?'

The owner blinked hard and his trousers discolored themselves with urine. Jacob barged past him and ripped the poster from the window.

'I see you've already pissed yourself, so let's keep this short n sweet. Open up that register and gimme everything you got!'

The owner's hands quivered. He tried to open the till but it jammed. Jacob crushed the owner's shoulder with his grip. He tried a second time and the register popped open.

'If at first you don't succeed... is what I call attempted murder,' said Jacob with a wry smile.

After Jacob snatched the money, he killed him by repeatedly bashing his skull off the counter.

~

The golden hues of dusk tinted the blue sky. The family stepped out from the car and waded through the overgrown weeds. The house's lime green paint was chipped and a moldy porch chair swayed in the wind. The father opened the door, which had been savaged by termites, and a damp stench spewed outwards.

'Breathe it in family, that's the smell of vacation.'

Whilst everyone busied themselves in their respective rooms, the father hastily stashed his cash into some old cereal boxes.

'What's for dinner tonight dad?' asked Sara.

'How about me and Ryan catch some fish from the lake out back?'

Ryan followed him outside and they stared at the huge lake that reflected the sky like a mirror. The dad knelt and swooshed the water with his hand. He popped his finger in his mouth and tasted it.

'I'll never know what it is boy, but the fish in this lake always taste so good.'

~

On the far opposite side of the lake, officer Peyton urinated into the water and admired the ripples from his secretion. He flicked his cigarette into the water and zipped his fly. He crashed down on a log. Dozens of empty beer cans were scattered around, along with his detached gun. A voice murmured on his radio and he struggled to reach it. "Possible disturbance at the Indian casino."

'10-4. This is Peyton… I'll handle it.'

He scrambled to his feet and dusted himself. The sound of whimpering filled the air and he scowled at the bushes. He peered through and noticed a huge grizzly bear – its paw was bloodied and trapped in a razored trap. Surrounding it was a trio of cubs. Peyton started laughing and taunted the bear by throwing beer cans at it.

'God damn vermin,' he muttered. His radio muttered again. 'I'm on it!'

Neglecting his gun, Peyton stumbled to his car and sped towards the casino.

~

The last clouds of evening hung above the trees

like the branches had pierced them, and in the distance the lake glimmered gold by the falling sun.

Jacob splashed the lake water over his face and cleaned the specs of blood. A disregarded cigarette floated on the surface. Jacob pinched it out and threw it away in anger.

'Jesus Christ what is it with people destroying the beauty of this world?'

As he scooped away the litter, he discovered Peyton's handgun. But as he grasped it, a gut-wrenching cry tore through the bushes.

He trudged through the branches to investigate and met with the towering grizzly bear. Jacob brandished the gun and aimed. Just as he went to shoot, he stopped himself. 'Ah screw it!'

He knelt and with all his might preyed open the trap. The bear cried in agony and Jacob smiled as it limped back to its family.

Night fell, and Jacob traversed through the dense darkness. His eyes caught a flickering light and he laughed in the murky shade.

*

The father sipped a cold beer and tapped the porch light to stop it from blinking. He headed inside. A plate of burnt trout fish was in the center. The family tucked in and chewed loudly with their mouths open.

'This fish tastes like sandpaper!' said Ryan as he spat some bones to the floor.

The father sniggered.

'Perhaps you'd prefer cornflakes for dinner?' she questioned.

'How's that?'

'Don't play fool with me, I know all about your lil gambling down at the casino!'

The father blushed. Just as he went to respond Sara slammed her phone on the table.

'I didn't get the part! I didn't get the lead in the play!'

'What's the production? The fat swan?' joked Ryan.

Sara thumped him in the face and Ryan picked up a fork and threatened to stab her in the eye. As the father broke up the squabble, there was a loud knock on the door. The mother left the kitchen to answer it.

When she opened the door, a man was stood under the flickering porch light. Two moths danced atop his head and he smirked with his yellow teeth.

'Evening,' said Jacob brandishing the gun.

*

Jacob tied each member of the family up, and placed them in separate rooms. The mother was tied to a chair in the kitchen. Jacob yanked the masking tape from her mouth.

'You know what's been bugging me?' she asked.

'What's that?'

'How'd a handsome fella like you end up in the pen? You don't look so scary to me.'

'That's because I have a code.'

'An what's your lil code?'

'I only kill people that deserve it.'

'So then how'd you end up in prison?'

'My wife deserved it.'

'Pity… what she do?'

'Bitch could start an argument in an empty house.' Jacob took a swig of water from the jug. 'Never could love a woman anyhow.'

'Maybe you just ain't found the one.'

'Ain't no "one" person miss. You see a woman will go out and try snag a man who's all rough around the edges, then if she succeeds, god willing she'll try and tame him. Then when she's done turning him into a sack of shit – she won't know what to do with him no more. Then she'll go out and look for someone else and the dance continues. That's why I ain't got no woman… Large hearts just have a bigger surface area to be walked all over.'

The mother stared at him with a sour expression. Jacob stared despondent. He grabbed a knife and pressed it on her neck. 'I'm the man that's gonna cut your pretty little throat if you don't tell me where the money's hiding!'

'I'll tell you where the money is… as long as you let me come with you!'

Jacob grinned.

'I'm not sure how our paths crossed. Be it by miracle or some cosmic joke… But one thing I do know is – I ain't never met a family like yours.'

The mother sat up in the chair and Jacob reproduced his gun. 'Your husband has no purpose and don't even get me started on your kids.'

'Well how's you think I feel? Cooped up all day with em! That's why I wanna start something new, something fresh, with you.'

Jacob's hair fell in front of his eyes.

'Truth is, I already done killed your family. I did

em all quick. Bullet to the back of the head! Don't worry, they all went smiling like a dead pig in the sunshine… You'll be next if you don't say where the money is.'

The mother tilted her head towards the cupboards.

'Check the cereal boxes. All the money should be there. Now untie me!'

Jacob ripped open the cupboards and shooed away the cockroaches. Inside the cereal boxes were wads of cash.

'Ah, a good woman is hard to find!' said Jacob as he untied her.

The mother ruffled her hair and stood all giddy.

'We can drive off into the night! Maybe stop at the casino. I can be like your lady luck. Better yet, let's rob the casino! We could be like that bank-robbing couple, what were their names? Jekyll and Hyde!'

Jacob leapt at her the way a cat would a mouse. He shoved his tongue down her throat and brushed her neck with his stubble. The mother leaned back on the table and they passionately kissed. A warm rush flowed through her body and he let go of his embrace to catch his breath. The mother fixed her hair, and as she smiled softly, Jacob drew his gun and shot her right between the eyes. He snatched the car keys, and scrammed for the door.

As Jacob stashed the trunk, a loud voice bellowed.

'Jacob! Put your hands up!'

Jacob smiled and scratched his stubble.

'Officer Walker.'

'Three days I spent in the hot sun tryna find you!'

Jacob scrunched the cash in his fists.

'What can I say officer, I love the honey but I run from the bees.'

Peyton peered in the trunk. The huge stash of money almost sobered him. He raised his firearm and fired at Jacob's feet. Jacob dodged and crawled behind the porch chair.

'Careful officer, snakes recoil before they strike!'

Jacob fired back blindly. Peyton opened the car door and used it as a shield. Foliage from the branches fell around him and bullets lodged themselves into the car. It went quiet for a moment and Peyton reemerged. Again Jacob relentlessly fired, shattering the car's wing mirror. Again it went quiet. Peyton realized Jacob was out of ammo. He sprung up and fired. The bullet tore apart Jacob's shoulder and he crashed to the dirt. Peyton limped over and held him up.

'I ain't sending you back to the joint. Someone like you deserves to die!'

Jacob clasped the gun with his hands and moved it in front of his heart.

'Sweetening the poison won't make it any less deadly. You and me, good and evil, light and dark - we'll always be intertwined. Man's life is linear, we're born and we move inexorably towards death. Pull the trigger, let me enjoy death's cold embrace!'

The gunshot echoed into the night and Jacob thudded to the floor. Peyton leaned on the bonnet and panted. He glared at the cash and smirked.

'This is officer Peyton Walker – I'd like to report a multiple 187!' He raised his gun in the air and fired.

'Shots fired! I repeat shots fired! Location is south of the residential woodland housing!'

Without waiting for a response he grabbed the cash and headed into the woods. Sweat poured from the side of his head, and thoughts of becoming rich filled him with excitement. He lit a small fire and dug a hole next to a large distinct oak tree.

After Peyton buried the loot he laughed to himself and took a successful drag of his cigarette.

The embers of the fire flickered into the night and the chirping of crickets filled the silence. The nocturnal serenity held him, and as he admired the blanket of stars, which now seemed ever radiant, he was killed by a bear, who believed he was a threat to its family.

Crossovers

Some of the stories also paid homage to other tales in the collection. I hope you spotted them all!

Stainless Steel Ride

Edmond spots the restaurant: Qantam Ad Luna.
Under The Moonlight She Flourishes.

Nothing To Declare

Gordon spots Heather in the airport.
A Woman's Work Is Never Done.

Queen of the Night

Bella picks up Nate who mentions Jack Redsky.
Under The Moonlight She Flourishes.

Lydia & Livia

Aunt Ophelia sells her fur coat to Mrs. Holland.
A Woman's Work Is Never Done.

Under The Moonlight She Flourishes

Laura references Vergil's pharmaceutical company. *Nothing To Declare*.

A Woman's Work Is Never Done

Mrs. Holland mentions her fur coat from Ophelia. *Lydia & Livia*.

A Most Unusual Day

The storeowner mentions the deaths in the dessert. *Queen of The Night*.

Acknowledgements

As this is a short story collection, I'm going to keep this section short and sweet. I would like to thank the following people for their everlasting support.

Paul Khanna, *for his wisdom and guidance.*

Gilbert Kyem, *for his friendship and laughter.*

Nilan Dharmadasa, *for his constructive advice.*

Victor Njimezi, *for his enthusiasm and spirit.*

Roald Dahl, *for paving the creative path.*

Ralph Waldo Emerson, *for sage advice found throughout his writing.*

Social Media

I love hearing from you so please stay connected with me on social media

Facebook: StrangeTalesStory

Twitter: @DJoaquimSilva

#StrangeTales

Beyond The Luna

The stars no longer twinkle and the moon is broken. Embark on a danger filled quest and help solve the mystery that lies Beyond The Luna.

Echo In The Forest

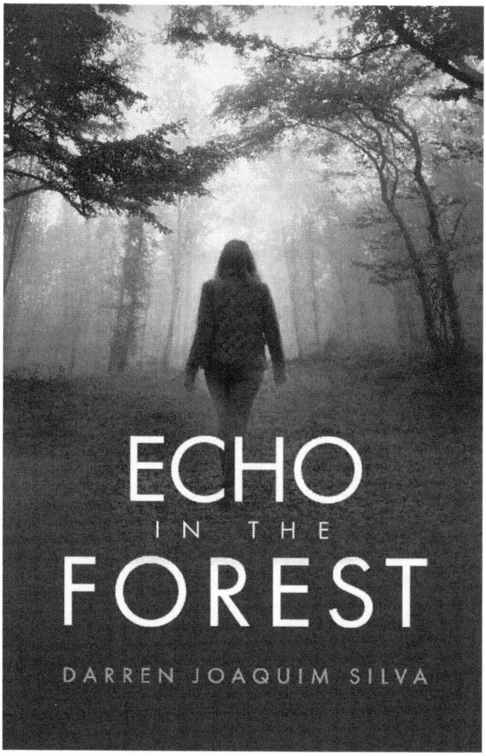

It was the perfect birthday for Echo until the disappearance of her parents left her orphaned and alone. Struggling for answers, she ventures into the very place her parents warned her about, the forest.

But an unspoken darkness looms under the trees, delighting in her sorrow, and biding its time.

Stainless Steel Ride

On the way to serve a death penalty, a convict recounts his life looking through the windows of the prison bus.

Nothing To Declare

Whilst their flight is delayed at an airport, two passengers strike up a very interesting conversation about life.

Queen of The Night

Driving alone through the desert, a woman decides to go against her intuition and pick up a shady hitchhiker.

Careless Talk Costs Time

A New York taxi cab driver becomes obsessed with a particular passengers life story.

Lydia & Livia

Twin sisters grow up enmeshed in a rivalry. After years of living in the others shadow one decides enough is enough.

Under The Moonlight She Flourishes

A man takes his girlfriend to a lavish restaurant in order to propose, but are his intentions of everlasting love real?

The Man Who Followed Himself

A mans quest to find the perfect gift for a woman, ends up with him finding much more.

A Woman's Work Is Never Done

A determined woman gets more than she bargained for, when she thinks her husband is committing adultery.

A Most Unusual Day

On a sunny afternoon, the dysfunctional lives of a family, a cop, and a killer all intertwine.

Printed in Great Britain
by Amazon

60096910R00095